THE BLOOD CRIES OUT FOR VENGEANCE

J.P. MADROX

THE BLOOD CRIES OUT FOR VENGEANCE

Angelico Press

First published in the USA
by Angelico Press 2023
Copyright © J.P. Madrox 2023

For information, address:
Angelico Press, Ltd.
169 Monitor St.
Brooklyn, NY 11222
www.angelicopress.com

paper   978-1-62138-946-0
cloth   978-1-62138-947-7

Book and cover design
by Michael Schrauzer

For Jean-Luc Beauchard

L'anima santa, che 'l mondo fallace fa manifesto

"If you permit the young to be viciously brought up and their characters steadily corrupted from early years, and then at length punish them for doing as adults what they have been destined for since childhood, what is this but turning people into criminals and then punishing them for being such?"
~ Raphael Hythlodaeus

"The way up and the way down are the same."
~ Eleusinian Mystery

"Bind his hands and feet and cast him into the outer darkness where there will be wailing and grinding of teeth."
~ The Gospel According to Matthew

AUTHOR'S NOTE: CATHOLIC NOVELIST, AMERICAN NOVEL

Have you also noticed that it's gone out of fashion for novelists to open with an Author's Note? I was struck by this a few weeks back when I returned to *The Brothers Karamazov* for the first time since I began writing this novel in the now-long-dead summer of 2016. That work, you no doubt remember, begins with a few exegetical remarks identifying Alexei Karamazov as the novel's unexpected hero and setting the stage for the tragicomedy to come. What inspired me to return to it after all these years? I wish I could say it was one of those arbitrary emotions like jumping off a cliff or falling in love. In truth, however, it was something I read, something that provoked me, shook me from my dogmatic slumber and forced me to consider things anew—myself most of all. I won't go on about the book that so stirred me it might fairly be credited with having brought me into being. (The subtle reader will have guessed it already.) I will only say that it caused me to reexamine my role as author and to recognize the need to give at least a cursory account of myself and my undertakings. Authorial anxiety and postmodern theory be damned. I am this book's author and this is my peremptory note.

I suppose I ought to begin by addressing what led me to write the work you now hold in your hands. Its influences are obvious enough. Cormac McCarthy, to whom this novel owes so much that it might be considered the ugly offspring of the bastard stepchild of his fifth cousin twice removed, once told the *New York Times* that "books are made out of books, the novel depends for its life on the novels that have been written." What he neglected to mention, however, is that books are also made of books unwritten, novels conceived, mulled over, and forgotten, existing nowhere but in mind or secret recesses of a single storyteller's heart. I bring this up because, while the derivative elements of this novel should be plain to every literate and even semi-literate reader in the English-speaking world—it simply lifts, for example, Dostoevsky's sacrificial ethic, McCarthy's bloody aesthetic, O'Connor's strange religion, Eco's biblical plotting—what is not seen and, indeed, cannot be seen, is the multiverse of possible works out of which this book was made.

Originally written as a screenplay called *Ex Nihilo*, *The Blood Cries Out for Vengeance* has suffered more revisions over the past 6 years than I'd care to admit. (And not always, it should be noted, for the better.) Whether the iteration you currently possess is the best of all possible works is not for me to say. But, as my favorite living aphorist recently observed, "Every writer reaches that point where it no longer matters if the work is good so long as it is done." Three cheers for literary pith! The problem is, I'm not sure I've reached that point. I don't know that I ever will. One can always go on revising. What I am sure of is that this work is done with me. Its hour has come. It must stand on its own and exist for itself or be choked to death by my meddling hands. Books, like boys, can be tyrannized by their fathers. Few escape the despot's shadow.

If I'm honest with myself, I have to admit that in me the destructive impulse runs deep. I'm a bit like Cronus, ready to devour his young. That's because I, like many artists, have an inordinate sense of self. What I demand from my work is not perfection, but greatness, something that can live up to the idol I've created in the unreality of my mind. There are two expressions of narcissism to which every author is subject. The first is to want to burn that which one has written, to prize oneself over one's creation, to see that which one has made as something low, unworthy, a dereliction, a source of embarrassment and shame. The second is to not want to burn that which one has written, to choose instead to force it out into the world, insist upon its merit, and thus insist upon one's own merit as well. Of the two heresies, I find the latter to be less pernicious, if only slightly. That's because when one allows one's work to be published, one abnegates control. A book in the world is a thing. It can be examined and probed at and reflected upon. It can be questioned. It can be ignored. It can be interrogated. It can be torn limb from limb and fed to a pack of frenzied maenads. If anyone condescends to read it, it will be criticized. It exists and, in so far as it exists, it exists for others. Regardless of what the author wants, a book has a life of its own.

Here is my struggle. I love my books in my mind—but how will I feel about them when I know how others feel about them? Will I go on viewing them as I do now, as a doting mother might view her children? Or, like an overbearing father, will I wish I had kept them locked away, safely sheltered from the light and the eyes—the claws—of others? Am I capable of loving? Do I love only with my head but not my blood, not in my guts, not with my heart and the life it sends coursing through my veins? Is my love given freely, without condition? Or am I just a man, as subject as anyone to the barbs and arrows of the many?

Unriddling this inner tension is made more complicated by the fact that I stand at an unfrequented crossroads. As an author, I am consciously Catholic and semi-consciously American—a coupling as paradoxical as the hypostatic union. My thinking is at once traditional and rebellious, communal and individualistic. The American in me says liberty. The Catholic, authority. The American, live free. The Catholic, thy will. The American, pursue happiness. The Catholic, take up your cross. These contradictions mark my characters as well, many of whom find themselves caught in similar webs. Ignacio, for example, is thoroughly American. He is at bottom a moralist who wants to believe in reformation. He's undergone a great awakening. He hopes for second chances. He wants to make himself anew. But so too is he dogged by a kind of crude, pious fatalism. He stands in need of grace. He's incapable of change. His salvation comes from without. Original sin hangs over everything. He is, in short, as Catholic as Augustine.

In this way, my characters (and I) exist in a space from which many Catholic Americans—or is it American Catholics?—have been eager to escape, a space in which no one really fits. I suspect, as I write this, that I will be misunderstood. Of course, Catholics have ascended to the heights of American life, both politically and artistically. Catholics have played an inordinate role in the shaping of this country, particularly with regards to its cultural imagination. Gone are the days when a Jesuit could be put to death for simply setting foot in Massachusetts (though I know more than a few academics from the Bay State who would be eager to resurrect that law if they could). What I am not doing when I identify this rift between the Catholic and the American is giving voice to the decadent persecution complex that exists among so many Christians today and is a symptom of comfort and success and, more than anything else, an assurance that no such persecution currently exists. No, what I am speaking of is a psychological, or, rather, a spiritual dilemma. What I'm trying to articulate is the antagonism that exists within the self, a self caught in the tension between two antithetical ways of existing in the world, the declaration of independence and the way of the cross. That such a conflict can exist in the heart of a single human being is a mystery. That, recognizing the conflict, one might seek its intensification rather than its dissolution is an absurdity. But books are made of absurdities. There would be no literature if life made sense.

Having come to the end of my thoughts on this topic, it is right, I suppose, to conclude my Author's Note. Reading it now, I see that it says very little about the book you're preparing to read and perhaps nothing at all. And so, decency compels me to admit that books are better nowadays when readers refuse to indulge their authors and won't allow them to pretend to be that which they are not—philosophers, literary theorists, interpreters of their own works. Writing this was a mistake. Allowing it to stand is a bigger mistake still. And yet, some mistakes are better left uncrossed out. Like a character who, once created, refuses to be erased, this note now stands as a signpost, a witness against me, warning friend and foe alike that its author is a second-rate artist and a fourth-rate thinker. Very well. I accept its condemnation. Every man is the child of his works.

J. P. MADROX
Feast of St. John of the Ladder
March 30, 2022

FOREWORD: WHO IS THE PRIEST? ❧

BY JAMIESON DE QUINCEY

> *"The street was like a movie theater and he felt like part of a movie, like a shadow, a ghost."*
> ~ Miguel de Unamuno, *Fog*

Don't be fooled, friends, by the seemingly self-deprecatory note appended to the start of this book by its author. Instead, read through such charming guises—that is, *see* through them by reading closely and reading well—to the man masked beneath. I begin with this warning because I, as one trained to read films, am no stranger to the power of appearance. Images are my wheelhouse. I think in moving pictures. And, having spent more time in front of the screen than is advisable for an otherwise healthy woman in her (blush) mid-30s, I possess a deep appreciation for stagecraft. That, I'm afraid, is what Madrox's opening salvo is. A bit of scenery. An artful getup. A theatrical prop. "Actors," observes Descartes before embarking on his illustrious career, "taught not to let any embarrassment show on their faces, put on a mask. I will do the same. So far, I have been a spectator in this theater which is the world, but I am now about to mount the stage, and I come forward masked." Such an admission might be made by every author preparing to foist her vision upon the world. Writers reveal themselves by donning disguises. Writers of fiction make masks of their characters. And, indeed, is this not just what Madrox confesses he has done?

Consider his prologue. Summed up in a few sentences, it says: This work may be unoriginal, its author may be inadequate, but at very least its protagonist is interesting. Ignacio makes this book worthwhile. He is the embodiment of a paradox. He is tension incarnate. And so, by the way—*am I*. Did you catch that, friends? Did you see how subtly he hinted that Ignacio's strengths are his own? That the priest's virtues are really his? When I read this, I was reminded of a little ditty I recently stumbled upon:

> I was made not for love,
> Not joy, not gladness from above,
> Not for wailing down below,
> Not rebellion, not for show,
>
> Not for sadness, not for pain—
> I was made to bear the strain.
> I live forever in-between
> Where gods and devils tear the seam.

Who would claim such a mantle? Who parade about with such shamelessness, such conceit? No, better not to let the embarrassment show on one's face, better to let one's characters bear the cross of one's self-adulation by masking oneself behind them. And then, if they are condemned, bound hand and foot and cast into the outer dark, well, at least it's they and not their author.

As I said above, I write on movies; and so, you'll have to excuse me if I offer a more cinematic, and less literary, introduction to this text. What you will find in the pages that follow, what I found when I read this book for the first time, is a work unmistakably marked by the influence of the 21st century American screen. In his Author's Note, Madrox identifies his forerunners as, among others, Hemingway, McCarthy, and O'Connor. I would say he draws more from Tarantino, the Cohen brothers, Sam Mendes, and even Cary Joji Fukunaga than from any of those literary sources. This book reads like the screenplay for *No Country for Old Men* sandwiched between the opening scene of *True Detective* and the final scene of *Road to Perdition*. It steals its objective correlative from *Inglourious Basterds*—scalping symbolizes the destruction of reason—and, like in all Tarantino films, blood is its *leitmotif*. It is coarse, violent, and dialogue heavy. It runs at a breakneck pace. Camus famously called novels "philosophy in images." *The Blood Cries Out for Vengeance* is images in images, scenes that whirl past too quickly to be seen, yet leaving a noticeable trace. One gets the sense when reading this book that it is better suited for the screen. But here we have it on the page. How to make sense of the form?

One way of untangling this Gordian knot is to observe the mashed-up, hodgepodge nature of the entire text. It is both a novel and a film just as its protagonist is an atheist-priest in love with a prostitute-saint, hunted by a murderer-mystic. Its characters live between faith and doubt, death and new life, conversion and an inescapable compulsion to repeat. Everything, this novel seems to shout, is at least double; our interpretations, rooted as they are in opposite values, break down before the brutal beauty and beautiful brutality of a world that nails its creator to the cross. The cross. It's a perfect image of such strange contradictions. God's bleeding heart situated at its center. The crown of his head pointing up toward the heavens, his eyes cast down on the earth, his arms outstretched to contain all things and yet, restrained, nailed to the wood so they can embrace nothing, hold nothing, comfort no one. What an odd sort of god this dying god is. What an unsettling incongruity. A thing both intimate and alien, in which we find ourselves and see that which we hope never to be.

The epigraph with which I open this Foreword comes from a book that proposes a new style of writing, a new literary form. The *nivola*, declares Victor Goti, is like a novel except it is dialogue heavy, character rich, in

which characters emerge from dialogue, are character-
ized by speech, by their ability to articulate themselves
in stories, stories told to one another and to themselves,
even to their dogs. The *nivola* is a more artful screenplay in which characters come to life not merely on
the page but in the world by speaking for themselves,
speaking themselves into being. It is my contention that
The Blood Cries Out for Vengeance embodies this *nivolian*
spirit, except that its author betrays himself and his
characters in his opening remarks, revealing Ignacio
de la Cruz—the *radiant one* who happens also to be
of the cross—to be fashioned in the image and likeness
of his author, no more than a mask for his god. That
doesn't make him any less real, but it does, perhaps,
make him a bit less original, a bit more contrived, and
so, in the end, a bit less himself.

Still, if we take that paradoxical image of god
on the cross seriously and admit that perhaps even
lesser artists can approach its sublimity then we'll be
forced to read this *nivola* against its author, against
his words and wishes, against the interpretation he
has attempted to impose upon this work in advance
by penning that disastrous Note. My advice to you,
dear friends, when reading this book would be to
ignore Madrox entirely. Forget about his Author's Note.
Forget everything you know of him. Dive in and see
where the story and the characters take you, how the
world in which they live unfolds. If you do that, if
you forsake the creator for the sake of the character,
then you may end up finding—as even the inventor
of the *nivola* came to appreciate—that "Characters
often end up toying with their author." And that is
because they have lives of their own.

THE BLOOD CRIES OUT FOR VENGEANCE

"You believe in god then, padre?"

"I believe in the absence of god."

"How's that?" said the lawman and he gave him a straight look.

The priest did not respond.

"You know," the lawman continued, "we was trackin this outlaw once. Jimmy the Younger. Ever hear a him?"

"I heard of him."

"Used to terrorize the border towns—thievin and killin and fuckin as he liked. When we finally caught him, he took as many a us as he took years. Only one thing to do with a man like that."

The priest grunted.

"Supposed to be strung up at daybreak. But sheriff—he's a Christian man. Believes in mercy. Told him we'd wait til his sister showed."

The priest drew on his cigar and the smoke and ash sat in the back of his throat.

"Now her train was due in at noon. But it was late. And the town folk, they was gettin restless. Done waited long enough. By half past, the rope was snug round ole Jimmy's neck and the hangman had his hand on the lever. That's when a shout comes up from the crowd. 'Repent Jimmy! Repent! It ain't too late! God'll forgive ya!' There's little sis. All in hysterics."

The priest exhaled and the smoke died in the dead desert air.

"Know what Jimmy did next?" the lawman continued. "He looked down at her. Looked straight into them big, sad eyes. Then, cool-as-you-like, he says: 'Darlin, who gonna forgive him?'"

The red Arizona sun was just rising over the plains.

The two rode on in silence for nearly ten miles before coming to a stop at the base of a small, dry ridge. There stood an old wooden fence, rotted and splintered. It had been used by some shepherd or herdsman decades before to keep his flock from wandering. Now it was ant-bitten and sun-beaten and forgotten. It served as little purpose as the dry stones that grew drier under the hot desert sun.

The priest looked at the man.

"Well," he said. "There it is."

"There it is," the lawman said.

They had come together from morning mass. The priest gave mass every morning in an old Spanish church. It was built by Jesuits some two centuries before. Then, when the crown stopped trusting the Jesuits, it was abandoned. Then the Dominicans took over. They ran it for a while before being butchered by a pack of apache. Or at least that's what people said. Then it was abandoned again. Around the turn of the century, it was struck by lightning and nearly burned to the ground. It stood in ruins for fifty-some-odd years. Then, when Ignacio de la Cruz was ordained as Fr. Ignacio de la Cruz, he petitioned the bishop and was granted permission to rebuild the church and offer daily mass. He said mass every morning at dawn, before sunrise. The town was small and there were few parishioners. Once someone had asked him what he'd do if nobody showed—didn't it defeat the purpose to give mass with no one to receive it?

"It don't make no difference," he said. "There's someone who needs it, whether you can see him or not."

The walls of the old church were made of mud and clay. The air was fogged with incense. Statues, candles, crude religious art. A large wooden crucifix hanging over a stone altar. Sunlight broke in through windowless frames. The pews were mostly empty. A frail old widow sat up front, hands folded in prayer, head covered with a lace mantilla. She rocked back and forth and mumbled to herself. She had consumption and hacked and coughed throughout the service. The lawman had entered about halfway through and he stood in the back. He wore tan boots and tan pants and a metal badge that had once belonged to his father. He put his hands in his pockets and looked out of place. He waited for the mass to end before telling anyone why he was there.

The priest, Fr. Ignacio, had a deep, red scar that spanned the length of his face. His vestments were crimson and gold with an ornate gold cross stitched over the center. His hair was black, his skin brown and worn. He might have been forty. He wasn't sure. Judging by his earliest memories, he guessed that he'd been born around 1820. Both of his parents were dead before he could walk and he was raised by nuns in an orphanage outside of Mexico City. He had come to the States as a teen and had never gone back.

Throughout the service, Ignacio looked down at his hands and thought about what those hands had done and what they could do and what they might do still. He performed the rituals in silence—blessing, consecrating, genuflecting, raising host and chalice high in the air, breaking the host into the chalice and preparing to consume. He was assisted by a young altar boy, no older than ten. The boy, too, was an orphan. He had come west from Louisiana with his parents and younger sister. One day his mother and sister went missing. They were found a few miles off in the desert walking near one of the silver mines. The next day, it rained. And the day after that, they went missing again. A few of the local miners saw his mother take his sister by the hand, walk to the edge of a mineshaft, and jump in. They descended down into the darkness and it swallowed them like Jonah swallowed up in the belly of the whale. But they didn't come back out again. Later that week, the boy's father shot himself. He couldn't figure what else to do.

Ignacio recited the "Agnus Dei" and as he did the laity rose from their pews and approached. They knelt at the stone altar rail and received the host on their tongues. The lawman remained in the back, listening to the incantation, wondering what it meant.

After the final blessing, he walked up to altar.

"Take your hands out a your pockets," Ignacio said.

The lawman looked at him.

"This ain't no saloon. You should genuflect too."

"I'm a baptist," the lawman said.

"Baptists can kneel just as good as anyone else."

"I'll wait outside," the lawman said.

"You can talk to me here," Ignacio said.

"Sheriff sent me," the lawman said. "Got somethin he wants you to see."

"Now?"

"Now."

Ignacio removed his vestments, revealing a simple black cassock. It had brass buttons down the center and a black belt wrapped around the waist. It had a white collar and white cuffs underneath and he wore black boots and a black hat. Then he mounted his horse and followed the lawman out into the desert. They sat side by side on horseback and watched the red sun break over the ridge and reveal in brilliant colors the scene laid out before them. Ignacio listened to the man talk about the outlaw Jimmy the Younger and a cigar end burned between his teeth. In front of the horses was a dilapidated fence and in the air was the low, dull hum of horseflies circling and beating their wings and tied to the fencepost was a pale, slumped body.

A young boy—shirtless, shoeless, posed kneeling— was slouched up against the rotting wood. He was an orphan named Alexei who had gone missing several

4

months before. His hands were bound and folded together as if in prayer. His bare back was raw with whiplashes. His head stooped down against the post but the men could see his scalp pealed back revealing the white of his skull. Black blood pooled and congealed in the dirt beneath his knees. The bottoms of his feet were charred as if burned with fire. His eyes were open and serene, his lips cracked and dry. His tongue hung from his mouth like the tongue of a dead deer.

Ignacio climbed down from his horse, dropped his cigar butt to the ground, pressed it out with his foot, walked over to the body, and crouched next to it to take a closer look.

"You ever seen something like that?" the lawman said.

Ignacio took off his hat and ran his fingers through his hair.

"Ain't never seen nothin like that," the lawman said.

Ignacio touched the boy's cheek. Then he blessed himself, made the sign of the cross over the body, stood, returned to his horse, mounted it, and rode away.

❧✿❧

Ignacio tied his horse to a post, patted it twice on the nose, and followed the lawman into the county jail. They walked down a long hallway at the end of which was the sheriff's office. A small, black rodent scurried across the dirt floor and squeezed itself into a crevice where the floor met the wall. Ignacio spat and the lawman gave him a look.

"This ain't no saloon," he said.

Ignacio spat once more.

The hallway was lined with steel bars and caged up behind the bars were men. Black flies buzzed and hissed and flew in circles. Birds nested in the rafters. They squawked and shat down on the men and the men cussed and threw stones at them. One of the prisoners reached out from his cell as Ignacio walked past.

"Father!" he said. "Father!"

"Santino," Ignacio said.

He stopped and took the prisoner by the hands.

"Do you still think of me?" the prisoner said. "Do you remember me in your prayers?"

"Each morning and every night," Ignacio said.

"I'm to be hanged," the prisoner said. "A week from tomorrow."

"Bear it with courage," Ignacio said. "The lord knows how you suffer."

"He forgot me," Santino said. "He forgot and left me here to die."

"He don't forget," Ignacio said. "Bear it. It's all you can do. Bear it and trust he don't forget."

"Alright," the lawman said. "Ain't no time for a powwow."

Ignacio turned to walk away.

"Don't leave me," the prisoner cried. "Don't let me die here alone!"

Ignacio stopped and walked back to the cell. He pulled a pair of wooden beads from his pocket and handed them to the prisoner.

"I'll be back before next week," he said. "I'll come to you. Until then, pray."

The prisoner looked down at the beads. His hands trembled.

Ignacio turned and walked away.

"Don't leave me," the prisoner cried. "Don't let me die alone!"

"What's the use, padre?" the lawman said. "Can't save everybody."

Inside the office the sheriff sat at a small, oaken desk scratching notes onto a piece of brown paper. He was tall and thin with a thick mustache and a wrinkled forehead. He sipped coffee from a metal cup and next to the cup was a bottle of whiskey that he used to sweeten the coffee and to steady his hand which tended to shake when he didn't want it to. He didn't look up as the men walked in and they stood just inside the doorway looking around the room.

"What's he doin here?" Ignacio said.

He pointed to the lone cell at the back of the office. There lay a man passed out drunk. He was a pale, stocky man with black hair and yellow eyes which hung open even as he slept. His fingernails were dirty and there was blood caked on his knuckles and on his shirt.

"Picked him up last night," the lawman said. "Drunk too much and ended up beatin the hell outta one a the whores over at ma'am's place. Damn near killed her."

"Which one?" Ignacio said.

"What's it matter?" the lawman said.

"Which one?" Ignacio said.

"Oh, right," the lawman said. "Forgot you had yourself a sweetheart, padre."

He laughed and patted Ignacio on the back. Then he turned and walked out.

"Sit," the sheriff said without looking up.

Ignacio walked to the desk and sat.

"What you make of it?"

"Someone murdered him," Ignacio said.

"Mmmm..." the sheriff said.

"Wasn't apache if that's what you boys are thinkin."

"Ain't thinkin nothin just yet," the sheriff said. "How you so sure?"

"Not their style," Ignacio said. "Scalp's a mess. Torn back—like with a stone. Would a been a cleaner cut.

7

Someone wanted it to look that way, maybe."

"Maybe," the sheriff said. "But maybe don't keep people from gettin up in arms. They'll want a posse. The usual."

"Who's seen him?" Ignacio said.

"You, me, the goatherd who found him," the sheriff said. "I got a few boys pullin him outta there now. Hopefully no one else. But word spreads. You know that."

"Mmm..." Ignacio said.

"Did you know him?" the sheriff said.

"I knew him," Ignacio said.

"Well?" the sheriff said.

"Name's Alexei," Ignacio said. "Thirteen probably."

"Last name?" the sheriff said.

"Ain't got none far as I know."

"One a your boys?" the sheriff said.

Ignacio nodded.

"Come to town about six months back," he said. "No family. Not a soul in the world. We took him in. He was a good worker. Good with his hands. Didn't talk much. Liked to listen. Liked to hear me read. Then one day he up and ran off. Ain't heard from him since."

The sheriff looked at him for the first time.

"Wasn't you worried?"

"Always worried, John," Ignacio said. "Ain't nothin to do but pray. Boys come and go. Join a gang or head west with gold in their brains. We shelter em as long as we can. Feed em. Give em some work. If they pick up and leave—well, they're in god's hands."

"Mmm..." the sheriff said. "He done good by this one."

Ignacio spat.

"Know what I think?" the sheriff said.

"I can guess, probably."

"I think them boys is lost," the sheriff said. "Ain't

8

worth your trouble."

"You wanted me for a reason?" Ignacio said.

The sheriff nodded.

"What was it?"

The sheriff poured some whiskey into his cup and offered the bottle to the priest.

Ignacio waved his hand in refusal.

"Thought you was a catholic man," the sheriff said.

"Bit too catholic of late," Ignacio said. "Why am I here?"

"You know them indians better than I do," the sheriff said. "Always have. Know what to look for. What to expect. And you know most everyone in this godforsaken town. Figured you could be a some use. Help me understand how this all happened."

"It wasn't apache," Ignacio said.

"Oh no?" the sheriff said.

"No," Ignacio said. "Looked almost like...like it was staged or somethin."

"Staged?" the sheriff said.

"Like whoever done it wanted us to find him that way. Like he propped him there on purpose. Almost like a statue."

"Now why'd he go and do somethin like that?" the sheriff said.

"Don't know," Ignacio said. "But when we first saw him, I knew I'd seen it before. Like I'd known the whole thing from before. The post, the sun, his back, that blood—all from somewhere before. Like I'd seen it all already."

"All due respect, father," the sheriff said. "You're talkin nonsense."

"Wasn't til we was ridin over that I realized where I had seen it before. And more than once. Time and again."

"What you after?" the sheriff said.

Ignacio pulled a black, leather-bound book from

the inside of his cassock. It was a small book of prayers. He thumbed through until he found what he was looking for and handed it across the desk.

"Christ almighty," the sheriff said.

The book was opened to an image of the scourging at the pillar. Christ's back was torn and bloody. He knelt, hands clasped tightly around the post, blood staining the ground beneath his knees.

"What's it mean?" the sheriff said.

"Not sure," Ignacio said. "Maybe nothin."

In the cell behind them, the man let out a deep groan.

"Which girl?" Ignacio said.

"Whore's a whore," the sheriff said. "Fuck if I know."

"Can I ask him?" Ignacio said.

"You can try," the sheriff said. "He's piss drunk. Ain't done nothin but moan and howl all night. Not a single word come from that mouth a his."

"What'll you do with him?"

"Wait til he sobers and send him on his way."

"Nothin more?" Ignacio said.

"For fuck's sake," the sheriff said. "What'd you have me do? It's the problem with you religious types. Always want your penance. Gotta get your pound a flesh."

"Could say the same a you, sheriff," Ignacio said. "Never known an officer a law to pass on the chance to hurt someone."

"You go straight to that hell you scare them women with."

"Come now, John," Ignacio said. "Don't be that way."

The sheriff put the bottle of whiskey to his mouth and drank off a gulp.

"You don't tell me how to be," he said. "I known you since before you took the cloth. Known where you got that scar. And I ain't forget it. I ain't forget what you is. Even if everyone else seem to."

Ignacio pushed his chair back from the desk and stood.

"If that's all," he said. "Good day, sheriff. I got sheep to tend."

He turned and walked out.

The sheriff ripped off another gulp of whiskey.

"Bet you do," he said. "Bet you do."

❧

Ma'am's was dirty—even by whorehouse standards. It was located just west of town by an old watering place where men stopped to water their horses and buy a quick lay. It smelled of booze and mildew and the faint tang of urine. There were cats living in the yard and in the house and under the floorboards and they mated and sprayed. They accounted for much of the smell but not for all of it and the smell was worse in the heat of the day when the sun beat down on the roof and the air was dry and still. The rooms were rarely cleaned and they stunk like sweat and menstruation. The girls were either fat or too skinny. They had greasy hair and stained outfits and makeup caked on their bruised or pockmarked faces. Every so often a rash would spread through the house and ma'am would have to close even though it cost her money and she hated doing it. She would hold off for as long as she could, quarantining the sick girls in the back bedrooms and hoping it would pass. It never did and it always got worse for having waited but she waited all the same.

Most of the girls were young and ugly. Teenaged or early twenties. Few stayed more than a couple of years. They stayed long enough to know they couldn't stay any longer. Then they'd pick up and leave. Head as far west as they could go. Every so often you'd hear talk about how one got herself killed in a bar or by some herders a few towns over. But mostly you didn't hear anything and you didn't much care.

As Ignacio approached, he saw a group of girls sitting out front playing with the feral cats and fanning themselves with makeshift fans. They talked and giggled and combed each other's hair.

"Here on a Sunday, father?" one said as he drew near.

"Want us to kneel for you?" said a toothless girl and she licked her tongue in circles around her toothless mouth.

They all laughed.

Ignacio looked up and his eyes settled on the youngest of the group. She was a skinny, flat-chested girl, no more than thirteen. Their eyes met and she looked away. He walked past and entered.

Inside, the house was damp and musty. It had a wood floor and wood tables and wood stairs that led to the bedrooms. There was a bar with whiskey and an old piano that hadn't been tuned since it was hoisted in through the large front window years before. There was a girl asleep, snoring in a chair. She was round, not fat, and pretty in an ugly sort of way. Another shaved her armpits and upper lip in front of a large, ornate mirror. The mirror had fingerprints and handprints all over it and the girl studied herself and dipped her razor in a basin of brown water and shaved.

The owner, who everyone just called ma'am, stood behind the bar wiping it with a rag. She was a thin, haggard, pathetic-looking woman with a wrinkled neck and small, wrinkled breasts. But she was far from pathetic. She'd killed or wounded more men than she could count and the number seemed to grow by the week. A miner or herdsman would enter drunk and looking for a fight and he would leave with a hole in his gut. She concealed a small, single shot Derringer pistol in her unmentionables and she was quick to use it. No one was quite sure how she got the money to open ma'am's but there were plenty of stories. They said she had killed her late husband, sold his land, moved out west, shacked up with an indian fellow, killed him too, sold his scalp, and used his land on the outskirts of town to build a brothel. Most of that was untrue of course. But she let people believe what they wanted so long as they paid for their whiskey and their lay.

"Father," she said. "A little early in the day ain't it?"

"No games, ma'am," Ignacio said. "Who was it?"

"Always so serious," she said. "When you gonna loosen up?"

"Not Maryellen," Ignacio said. "Say it wasn't her."

"You know," ma'am said, "it ain't too often that a girl here takes a likin to one of our customers. Usually such brutes. But she likes you. And I see why. So protective. The protective priest... It's bad for business."

"Where is she, ma'am?" Ignacio said.

"She restin," ma'am said. "Needs to get herself together for tonight. I ain't losin out on a night's work. That's for damn sure."

"Where?" Ignacio said.

"None a your goddamned business," ma'am said.

"Where?" Ignacio said.

"Fuck off, padre," ma'am said and she gave him a straight look.

She turned to walk away and when she did, Ignacio grabbed her by the wrist. She struggled and he tightened his grip. In an instant, her free hand was in her dress and back out, holding the Derringer pistol. Ignacio grabbed the gun by the barrel, pushed it down, and a shot rang out. The powder burnt the palm of his hand and the lead ball lodged itself in the wood floor at his feet.

"Goddamn it, ma'am!" he said without releasing his grip.

The girl sleeping in the chair jumped up and looked around. Then she ran out to get the others.

"Imagine that," ma'am said. "Killin a priest on a Sunday."

She laughed.

Ignacio let go of her wrist and backhanded her across the face.

She stumbled backwards and held up her hands to guard against a beating.

He pulled a bag of coins from his cassock and held it out.

"Now you're speaking my language," ma'am said, rubbing her jaw.

"That's for the rest a today and all a tomorrow," he said and he handed her the bag.

She shook it.

"Where is she?" he said.

"Upstairs," she said. "In her room."

Ignacio took a handkerchief from his cassock, wrapped it around his palm, and walked to the stairs. A crowd of girls came rushing in to see what had happened.

"Father," ma'am called after him.

He turned and looked at her.

"Won't the bishop be upset to learn how you're spendin his money? Usually stops by when he's in town. Hate for one a my girls to let your secret slip...on accident."

"You tell him what you want," Ignacio said. "He got his own sins to worry about."

He turned and ascended the stairs.

"Alright," ma'am said to the girls. "Back outside. You ain't attractin no business crowdin in here like a bunch a toadies."

The girls filed out.

Ma'am emptied the bag of coins on the bar and began to count.

He paused a moment outside the door. Then he knocked and waited.

"Who's there?" said a voice from inside.

"Maryellen," he said. "Open up."

"Father," she said. "Go away."

"Open up," he said.

"Please," she said. "I don't want you to see."

Ignacio stood outside not knowing what to do. He raised his hand and touched it to the wood. Then he turned and walked back down the hall toward the stairs.

The door opened.

He turned and walked back.

When he entered the room, he found her standing with her back to him looking out the window. He closed the door.

"Maryellen," he said.

She sighed.

He walked up behind her and put his hand on her shoulder.

"You know, I been readin my bible," she said. "The one you gave me."

He remained silent.

"'He'll wipe the tears from their eyes, and there won't be no more death, no more pain. What's old's done passed away.'" She paused. "You believe that, father? You believe them words?"

"Maryellen," he said.

"'And the one on the thrown'll say, 'Behold, I make all things new.''"

She turned and faced him and he saw her bruises for the first time. Her face was swollen and marred and she looked like she had been beaten half to death. There were tears in her eyes and she had welts down her arms and bruises on her shoulders and her

15

stomach and on her back.

"Maryellen," he said.

She looked away.

"Maryellen," he said.

He reached up to touch her cheek but she turned and would not let him.

❦

He spent the rest of the day at the brothel lying next to her on a small, straw mattress. She slept on and off but he didn't sleep at all. He just lay there, staring at the ceiling, running his fingers through her hair. Her hair was reddish blonde and it was wavy. It smelled like perfume powder and lavender and it curled in the back. She was plain and beautiful with freckles and red cheeks. She wore a white dress which matched her pale, white skin and she was barefoot with little nub toes and white toenails. When she woke, it was dark outside and dry thunder cracked in the distance but there was no rain.

"What I wouldn't give to kiss you," he said.

"Kiss me," she said. "Just this once."

"No," he said. "Once is all it'd take."

"And what if it is?" she said.

He sighed.

"I know," she said. "I know."

They lay there in silence.

"And if I did," he said. "I don't suspect you'd want to be with the type a man who can't keep his word."

She thought about that.

"No," she said. "I don't suspect I would."

He ran his fingers through her hair and she nestled her head on his chest.

"I should go," he said.

"Stay," she said.

"I should go," he said and he got up.

"When will I see you again?"

"I paid ma'am enough for you to have tonight and tomorrow off," he said. "Don't let her put you to work."

"I appreciate that," she said. "I really do."

He walked to the door.

"Father," she said.

He waited.

"Ya think we'll ever be together?"

"'At the resurrection they neither marry nor are given in marriage but are like angels in heaven,'" he said.

"What's that mean?" she said.

"I don't know," he said. "Been tryin to figure that one out."

"I hope it means we'll be together," she said.

He looked down at his feet.

"Remember me tonight," she said. "In your prayers."

"Remember me in yours," he said and he walked out.

❧

When he got to the church, it was dark and empty. The moon outside was full and bright and moonlight broke in casting oblong shadows on the walls. The wind blew through the windowless frames and the candles flickered and danced. He walked to the altar and stood for a long time looking up at the wooden god nailed to his wooden cross. He thought about Alexei and about how he died and how dead his cheek felt to the touch and he knelt to pray.

The door at the back of the church creaked open and a gust of wind whipped through. A cold chill shot down Ignacio's spine but he ignored it and kept his head bowed low.

A man entered through the open door and walked down the center aisle. His footsteps were slow and deliberate as if each one had been considered and planned out in advance. He came to a stop a few feet from Ignacio and gazed up at the cross.

"I don't believe," he said.

Ignacio turned and looked at him with surprise.

"I don't believe."

It was the man from the cell in the sheriff's office. He was calm and collected and he was wearing a new shirt. He had rid himself of the one stained red with Maryellen's blood.

"Doubt's a part a faith," Ignacio said and he rose to his feet. "Even the lord doubted. He thought he'd been abandoned. And he was the son a god."

"Heard you wanted to talk to me," the man said.

"I did," Ignacio said. "I do."

"I wanted to talk to you," the man said.

"That girl you beat up," Ignacio said.

"I wanted to talk about faith," the man said. "About the cross."

"Alright," Ignacio said.

"I don't believe," the man said.

"You come to mass," Ignacio said. "I seen you once or twice."

"I don't believe," the man said.

"Is that why you don't take the host?"

The man continued to stare at the wooden crucifix.

"Ask the lord for the faith you seek," Ignacio said. "He'll show you who he is."

"No," the man said. "That ain't it."

"What then?" Ignacio said.

"He's god," the man said. "I know that. And he died. I know that too. Had to die. Had to cause he loved. Can't call it love if ya won't die."

Ignacio cleared his throat.

"And I damn well bet he came back again," the man said. "The stubborn prick. Ain't much of a god if he can't do that."

"That's true enough," Ignacio said.

"But I don't believe, father. I don't believe. Always get hung up on the details. One detail in particular. Ya know what that is?"

"No," Ignacio said. "I don't."

"What's the name a the one who took him down from that cross?"

"Joseph of Arimathea," Ignacio said.

"Joseph of Arimathea," the man said. "Well, there it is."

"There it is," Ignacio said.

"You believe that, father?" the man said. "You believe in Joseph of Arimathea?"

"I believe," Ignacio said.

"No," the man said. "You ain't believe it neither."

"Who are you?" Ignacio said.

"You seen too much to believe," the man said. "Ain't that so?"

Ignacio coughed into his hand.

"You lived too long."

"Not sure what you're after," Ignacio said.

The man nodded.

"You are," he said. "You know just what I mean."

"Well," Ignacio said. "If I do..."

"Before you came here," the man said. "Before you took the cloth."

"What of it?" Ignacio said.

"I'm from Texas too," the man said. "Born near San Augustine. Spend some time down by Galveston way. Your name's pretty well known in them parts."

"I left Texas a long time ago," Ignacio said. "Whatever stories you heard—they about a different man."

The man nodded.

"I suppose that's true," he said. "But that different man ain't dead. He's buried but he ain't dead."

"He's dead," Ignacio said.

"You done your share a travelin," the man said. "Ain't that true?"

"What if I have?" Ignacio said.

"How many people you think you've met in your life?" the man said. "Five hundred? Thousand?"

"Maybe a thousand," Ignacio said. "Maybe more."

"Out a all them people," the man said, "not one Joseph of Arimathea. Ain't that right?"

"There's somethin off about you," Ignacio said. "I could tell when I saw you there. Knew it the first time you was in mass too. Somethin missin. Somethin behind your eyes."

"Not a single one," the man said. "Tell me, father— you know one man good enough to take his god down from that cross? You know one man loves enough to do that?"

"I know your type," Ignacio said. "Seen you before. Somethin not right with them eyes."

"No," the man said. "You ain't believe. You know what it means to take him down. You know what it means to push them nails back through his hands, to force that twisted steel back through his lifeless hands. You know it's too much."

"This what you came here for?" Ignacio said. "To talk this nonsense?"

The man shook his head.

"No," he said. "Came to tell you I was leavin town. You might not see me for a little while."

"Where you goin?"

"Places to go," the man said. "Heard you wanted to see me. Came here out a respect."

"That girl you beat up," Ignacio said.

"I know," the man said. "It was a mean thing to do. Did it out a meanness. Wasn't the booze or nothin else. Just wanted to be mean."

Ignacio nodded.

"I can understand that," he said.

Then he looked the man square in the face.

"You touch her again," he said. "I'll kill you with

20

my own hands."

"I believe that," the man laughed. "Now there's somethin I do believe."

"Believe it," Ignacio said. "It's the gospel truth."

The man turned and walked down the aisle and he exited the church.

Ignacio watched him go.

When the door closed shut, he looked up at the cross and down at his hands and he let out a low sigh. Then the wind howled and beat against the door and he knelt down and returned to his prayers. And when the morning came, he was still there on his knees before the altar. He had not moved or slept all night.

Each morning, the altar boy climbed the stone stairs that led to the bell tower of the church, pushed open the wooden door at the top, and tugged the rope that rang the bell that signaled the start of mass and the dawning of a new day. He always paused after pulling the rope and looked out at the quiet Arizona desert—the first rays of sun spread like fingers across the land. The sky looked cursed, he thought, as though chidden of god; and he cursed the sun and sky for bringing a new day. Then he descended the stairs and met Father Ignacio in the sacristy. There he prepared the chalice and the bread and helped Ignacio into his vestments and opened the missal to the day's readings. He assisted Ignacio throughout the mass and, after the final blessing, processed out with his hands folded tight. He was a young boy and he had experienced much suffering and he was about to experience more.

After morning mass, Ignacio and the altar boy stood outside greeting the few churchgoers in attendance as they made their exit. The altar boy looked up at the god-cursed sky and thought of how the sun used to hang low over the bayou in the heat of the day and how the air was moist and thick. He thought of his parents and of his sister and he closed his eyes and could almost see their faces, the image of his father's slumped body and the gun lying in the dry desert grass.

"Good day," Ignacio said to the frail, old widow as she hobbled out.

"Beautiful service," she said and she stopped to talk.

Ignacio nodded. "Glad to see you this mornin."

"And I'm glad to see you," the widow said. "Glad to have your prayers. Been havin such awful dreams.

Can't sleep all night. Not one lick. Jus kickin the bed-post and hollerin in my sleep. Jus rollin and tumblin the whole night long."

"Well..." Ignacio said.

"Some a them dreams," the widow continued. "Some a them nightmares been about you, father. The worst ones of all."

"About me?" Ignacio said and he laughed.

The widow nodded. Her face was grave.

"Dreamed you was gone," she said. "Lost at sea. Took a boat out in the middle a the night and ain't never come back. No one knew where you was. Then someone said you was swallowed up by a big, big fish. Said he saw you in its mouth and you was cryin for help, but ain't no help come. Said he saw its mouth close up around you, jus like round a little fly. Then it swim right off. And it ain't comin back."

Ignacio smiled.

"Well," he said. "I ain't got no plans to head out to sea."

"Dreamed about him too," the widow said and she pointed to the altar boy.

The boy looked away.

"Dreamed there was a nasty black fly and it was diseased and pusin from its mouth. And it was bitin everyone. And its bite was like plague and people was droppin to the ground and dyin in heaps and the bodycart couldn't fit no one else it was piled so high."

Ignacio coughed.

"That plague ruined us all. Every last one. All but him. The fly stung him. It stung him real good. But he didn't die. No, he turned into a fly himself, a mean-lookin drone, and he start buzzin and beatin his wings. And then it was his turn to do the bitin and he was happy to be doin it. He wanted to be doin it."

"Okay," Ignacio said. "You have a good day now."

The woman seized him by the hands and her eyes looked right through him.

"Father," she said. "I ain't know what's happenin. But I'm scared."

"It's okay," he said. "Ain't nothin to be scared a. You jus hang tight to the lord and make sure you're sayin your rosary and you'll be alright."

"You hear about that boy?" she said. "Round the same age as this boy, ain't he? Butchered up by them indians. Kill him. Scalp him. Leave him out there for the coyotes to pick at."

"I heard," Ignacio said and he looked at the boy.

The boy kicked the dirt with his foot.

"But it ain't nothin to fret over. Sheriff's got everything under control."

"He ain't," the widow whispered. "Ain't no one can control what's comin. I know that."

"You feelin alright?" Ignacio said. "You don't look so good."

"I seen him, father. I seen him in my dreams. And I ain't never want to see him again."

"What's that?" Ignacio said.

"The antichrist," the widow said. "I know what he looks like. I seen into his very eyes."

Ignacio looked at her intently.

"He's here," she said. "In town. Walkin among us. In human flesh."

The boy was getting upset.

The old woman broke into a violent coughing fit. She coughed and coughed and convulsed and shook.

Ignacio grabbed hold of her and she fell unconscious in his arms.

"Quick!" he said to the boy. "Run and get the doctor."

The doctor worked out of a small, dirty room with glass jars and vials on the walls. He had a table covered with rusty metal tools that he used to open people's flesh and see what was inside. He had three shrunken heads that he claimed to have purchased from a hunter who had traveled to the Brazilian jungle in search of exotic game; he actually got them from a scalper who stole them from a group of indians he murdered in cold blood. He had a fractured human skull and a tibia bone, both of which had once resided in a field slave in Georgia. In a jar by the door, he kept the remains of a human foetus submerged in a homemade mixture of embalming chemicals. Ignacio looked at the half-formed being and wondered who he might have been.

"You like it?" the doctor said.

Ignacio turned.

"Amazing what can grow in the human body."

"It is."

"There's so much we don't know," the doctor said reflectively. "But one day, we will."

"And if we do?" Ignacio said.

The old woman coughed. She was laid out on a bed in the corner of the room. She was unconscious with blankets pulled up to her face.

"What can be done?" Ignacio said.

"Not much," the doctor said. "Brain fever."

"Then there ain't no hope?"

"Convulsions. Delirium. Chills. Fits of terror. She'll be dead in an hour."

Ignacio blessed himself.

"Wonder what she looked like as a girl," the doctor said.

"How do you mean?" Ignacio said.

"My mind," the doctor said. "It wanders. Sometimes into unholy places, father. This woman was a girl once. What you think she looked like?"

"Like a girl," Ignacio said.

"But pretty though, yeah? A real looker."

"I don't know," Ignacio said. "Only known her of late."

"I got a girl," the doctor said. "A young girl. Planning on making her my wife."

"Marriage can be a blessin," Ignacio said. "And it can be a cross."

"Thirteen this October," the doctor said. "We'll be married next July."

Ignacio looked at him.

"I know what you're thinking," the doctor said.

"I'm sure you don't," Ignacio said.

"Don't you judge me," the doctor said. "At least not on a count of that."

"'By the standard you judge,'" Ignacio said, "'you condemn yourself, since you do the same thing.'"

"I like that," the doctor said. "That's nice."

"That's St. Paul," Ignacio said.

"A smart man," the doctor said. "But tell me, father—you ever done what I did?"

"Can't say," Ignacio said. "I'm not you."

"No, you're not," the doctor said. "That's for damn sure." And he laughed.

Ignacio stood and listened to the old widow breathe. There was fluid in her lungs and she gasped and coughed and choked on the air.

"I ever tell you about the married woman I been with?" the doctor said.

"No," Ignacio said. "And you don't have to."

"It was easy," the doctor said. "Too easy. First because she knew I was smarter than her. That always gets em. Smarter than her husband too. He's a blacksmith, the poor bastard. Only thing he knows how to do is beat metal with a hammer."

"I done some smithin," Ignacio said. "It ain't that easy."

"You want know what made it easiest of all?" the doctor said. "I kept on telling her how she didn't want nothing to do with me. Flattered her, you see? I said she was a faithful woman. A devout woman. A Christian woman. I said she loved her husband and there was nothing I could do to change it. I said I was no good, a real wretch. I said I ruined women and she wouldn't be a ruined woman—she was too proud for that. 'You're not interested in a man like me,' I said. 'You're a lady. You got your morals.'"

Ignacio coughed into his hand.

"When she kissed me," the doctor said, "I made out like it was my fault. 'There I go,' I said, 'taking advantage.' And when we—how to put it?—became one flesh… Well, she didn't even think she'd done anything wrong. She still believed she was a good, honest woman. It was me, she thought, who'd made her do it. You see what I'm saying, father? It was easy because she believed, because she wanted to believe. Needed to. She didn't like what was true."

There was a pause and the doctor's eyes seemed to gaze off at nothing in particular.

Then Ignacio coughed again and his cough broke up the silence.

"Well," the doctor concluded, "that's my story. How about it?"

"How about it?" Ignacio said.

"You think I feel shame?" the doctor laughed. "Shame's got nothing to do with it."

Ignacio walked over and looked down at the sick woman.

She convulsed.

Ignacio touched her cheek.

"One a the lucky ones, eh father?"

"How's that?" Ignacio said.

"Sheriff brought me a boy yesterday," the doctor said. "You seen him."

27

Ignacio nodded.

"What do you make of it?"

"Murdered," Ignacio said.

"Murdered?" the doctor laughed. "You don't mince words, do you? Sheriff said you don't think it was the indians."

"That wasn't no apache," Ignacio said.

"No, I don't think so neither," the doctor said. "You want to know the strangest part? That boy didn't die from his wounds. He was dead long before. What do you make of that?"

"I don't know," Ignacio said. "I don't know what to make of a lot a things."

"You don't know?" the doctor said. "Here I thought I was the one messing with you and now things are the other way around."

Ignacio shrugged.

"I tell you that someone killed that poor boy then scalped him and carved up his body with a bullwhip just for fun and all you can do is shrug and say, 'I don't know.'"

"What do you make of it?" Ignacio said.

"You want to know what I think?" the doctor said.

Ignacio nodded.

"I think whoever did that did it because he's got some wounds of his own."

"Might be," Ignacio said.

"Might be?" the doctor said. "No. Is."

Ignacio nodded.

"Let me ask you, father," the doctor said. "You hear a lot of confessions, yeah?"

"Some," Ignacio said.

"You ever known a man to sin who hasn't already been sinned against?"

"One tends to follow the other," Ignacio said.

"And if a man cheats," the doctor said, "usually it's because he's been cheated. And if he robs, it's because someone already took what's his."

"It can happen," Ignacio said.

"And if he kills," the doctor said, "it's because he knows he's dying. The thought a death makes him kill, either because he's scared and he doesn't want to feel scared or because he's dead inside and wants to feel alive."

"Seems right," Ignacio said.

"Then you tell me, father," the doctor said. "What kind of man marks up a body like that? What kind of man mutilates human flesh?"

Ignacio rubbed his hand along the side of his face. "What're you after?"

"You know what I'm after," the doctor said and he gave him a devilish wink.

"I want you to say it," Ignacio said.

There was a long, tense silence.

Then the doctor let out a laugh.

"Shit," he said. "Now I got you going, father. Just had to dig them spurs hard enough."

Ignacio did not respond. He rubbed his palm across the woman's forehead.

"No," the doctor said. "After giving that body a good exam, my money's on the apache. There's just no telling what those savages'll do."

Ignacio touched the woman's cheek and tried to comfort her as best he could.

Then the door flew open.

"You son of a bitch," said the lawman and he pulled out his gun.

❧❧❧

When they got to the prison, they found the sheriff pacing about in an empty cell. The door was slung open wide and the sheriff examined the room like he was examining the scene of a crime. They stood and watched as he studied the footmarks pressed down in the mud floor. He touched his fingers to the wall, pulled them back sticky with blood, and put them in his mouth to make sure it was blood. It was and it left an odd copper taste on his tongue. His mouth salivated and he licked his lips. Then he crouched down and examined the lock on the door. It had been busted open and pieces of the locking mechanism were spread out on the ground at his feet. He looked up at the two men standing in the doorway and let out a low, irritated grunt.

"You got somethin to tell me, father?" he said.

"No," Ignacio said. "I don't."

The priest stood in the doorway wearing handcuffs and shackles. The lawman stood behind him with his pistol pressed firmly against his back.

"How'd you explain this?" the lawman said and he gave him a shove.

"Put your piece away," the sheriff said. "This here's a holy man."

The lawman put his gun in his holster and spat.

"You boys want to tell me what's goin on?" Ignacio said.

"You know who lived in this cell not one day ago?" the sheriff said.

"Matter a fact I do," Ignacio said.

"And you know where he is now?" the sheriff said.

"Judgin by the open door and busted lock," Ignacio said, "I'd say he escaped."

"Don't be a smartass," the lawman said and he shoved the priest once more.

"What's this got to do with me?" Ignacio said.

"This man was set to be hung," the sheriff said. "You know that?"

"Yes sir, I do."

"A week from today," the sheriff said. "You know that?"

"I knew it," Ignacio said.

"What you think about that?" the lawman said.

"What's to think about?" Ignacio said. "You break the law, the law breaks you."

"That how it is?" the sheriff said.

"Far as I can tell," Ignacio said.

"How'd you manage to fare so well?" the sheriff said.

"I been broke," Ignacio said. "Been broke over the wheel."

"That so?" the sheriff said.

Ignacio spat.

"You gave him somethin," the lawman said and he grabbed the priest by the collar. "Handed somethin right through them bars."

"That's right," Ignacio said. "I did. Yesterday mornin."

"Somethin he used to bust this here lock," the lawman said.

"Now," the sheriff said in a stern tone. "How you expectin to catch a criminal when you go and tell him all we know?"

"He did though, sheriff," the lawman said. "I seen it. It's the god honest truth."

"You ain't need to see it," Ignacio said. "I jus told you I did. I gave him somethin. Yesterday mornin. Handed it right through them bars."

The lawman clenched his fist and punched the priest in the jaw.

It was a good punch but not that good and Ignacio spat and smiled.

"If I done somethin wrong," he said, "you tell me what it was. But if not, why're you hittin me?"

"You know what you did, you son of a bitch," the lawman said.

"Now," the sheriff said. "That'll be all. You step out and cool off. I'll take it from here."

"But sheriff..." the lawman said.

"That's an order," the sheriff said and he gave him a mean look.

"Yes sir," the lawman said and he walked out.

"Apologies," the sheriff said.

Ignacio rubbed his jaw.

"What you know about this?" the sheriff said.

"I don't know nothin, John," Ignacio said. "You know me."

"I do know you," the sheriff said. "I know what you're capable of."

"John," Ignacio said.

"This boy Santino," the sheriff said. "He a friend a yours?"

"Another one a the orphans," Ignacio said. "Not a bad kid. Not a good one neither. Knows how to get himself into a world a trouble."

"You used to know how to bust locks," the sheriff said. "Helped you out of a jam on more than one occasion."

"I still know how to bust locks," Ignacio said. "I just don't do it no more."

"You know how to bust this kind a lock?" the sheriff said.

"Sure," Ignacio said.

"You bust this lock?" the sheriff said. "You set that boy free?"

"No, sir," Ignacio said. "I did not."

"What'd you hand him through them bars?" the sheriff said.

"My rosary beads," Ignacio said. "A wood pair. Bought em near Tuscan just before my ordination."

"For Christ's sake," the sheriff said. "You expect me to believe that?"

"I'm a goddamned priest," Ignacio said. "You believe what you want."

"You know, this busted lock ain't half the mess I'm dealin with," the sheriff said.

"What else?" Ignacio said.

The sheriff stared at him as if trying to discern something.

"Where was you last night?"

"The church," Ignacio said.

"All night?" the sheriff said.

"All night," Ignacio said.

The sheriff grunted and he ran his hand through his hair.

"What happened, John?" Ignacio said. "Why am I in chains?"

"Come with me," the sheriff said. "Got somethin to show you."

Ignacio followed the sheriff through the prison in silence. They exited and walked toward the stable out back. Even at a distance, they could hear the colts snorting and kicking. Something had spooked them and the noise gave Ignacio an uneasy feeling in his gut.

"Where are you takin me?" he said.

The sheriff continued on without a word.

It was before noon but the midday sun already burned high and hot over the scorched desert earth. It cast no shadows, so directly did it beat down, and there was a terrible stillness in the air. The chains were heavy and tight on Ignacio's wrists and he panted as he walked. He looked up and saw two black vultures circling overhead. He began to suspect what he was going to see and he did not want to see it.

"You still got that club a yours?" the sheriff said.

"Yes, sheriff. I do."

"Ever miss swingin it?" the sheriff said.

"Not a day in my life," Ignacio said.

When they reached the stable, Ignacio heard the low, dull buzz of flies, and he swatted at something on his neck. The sheriff walked up to the stable doors and pushed them open. The two entered and Ignacio squinted as his eyes adjusted to the dark. Then he saw the hay and the horses and the scene before him. He stood in silence and thought of the last time he swung his club and a cold chill went up his spine.

❦

The last time Ignacio swung his club was a rain-soaked night in the summer of 1850 and he was soaked through with rain. The killing had been good for a long time and there was money in it. He hunted bounty through the Texas wilderness and recently a new trade took hold of the local economy and he was skilled enough to do it. He was good at what he did and he made his share of money and he used that money on nights like this to fill his belly with whiskey. He sat alone at a wood table in a local saloon, hair damp, clothes damp, boots off so his feet could dry. He sipped his whiskey and spat. Then a man entered. A man he recognized. A fellow bounty hunter. He was tall and thin with a thick black mustache and he was wet from head to heel.

"Been lookin for you," the man said from across the bar.

"Look no further," Ignacio said.

"Can I join you?" the bounty hunter said.

Ignacio nodded and the man walked over and sat at his table.

"You's a hard man to find," the bounty hunter said.

"Here I am," Ignacio said.

"You know why I'm here?" the bounty hunter said.

"I can guess, probably," Ignacio said.

"What'd you think the price is on your head?"

"Depends on who's settin it," Ignacio said.

"Couple a injun fellows," the bounty hunter said.

"They do not like you."

He thought about that.

34

"Maybe five hundred," he said,

"Higher," the bounty hunter said.

Ignacio smiled.

"That's good," he said. "Glad to know it."

"Can I ask you somethin?" the bounty hunter said.

Ignacio nodded.

"How'd you get that scar? It sure is an ugly thing, ain't it?"

Ignacio sipped his whiskey.

"This scar?" he said. "Had it most a my life."

"That so?" the bounty hunter said.

"Yes, sir," Ignacio said.

"But that ain't tell how you got it."

Ignacio spat.

"You bring some boys here with you tonight?" he said.

The bounty hunter nodded.

"Waiting outside," he said. "Ain't rash enough to come here alone. Ain't young enough neither."

"That's good," Ignacio said. "That'd be a mistake."

"Can I buy you another whiskey?" the bounty hunter said.

"That'd be nice," Ignacio said. "I'd appreciate it."

The bounty hunter signaled to the bartender and he came over and filled the glass.

"I'm glad it's you," Ignacio said.

"Me too," the bounty hunter said. "Always liked you."

"Glad to know it," Ignacio said.

"Always respected your opinion."

Ignacio sipped his whiskey.

"Can I ask you something else?" the bounty hunter said.

Ignacio nodded.

"What you think about the work we do? You think it's right?"

"How'd you mean?" Ignacio said.

"I mean, you think it's god's work?" the bounty hunter said.

Ignacio thought about that.

"No," he said. "I don't."

"That's what I thought," the bounty hunter said. "You know, I meet a lot a people in this country, say they're doin it for their god. Think cause it's the law that their doin somethin noble. Somethin right. But they ain't see it like we see it. The name a the law ain't the name a god. And he does his own work, far as I can tell."

"Seems about right to me," Ignacio said.

"No," the bounty hunter said. "The law's the people. Do it for them."

"And for ourselves," Ignacio said.

"And for ourselves," the bounty hunter said. "Can't forget that."

Ignacio sipped his whiskey.

"But maybe that ain't it neither," the bounty hunter said.

"How'd you mean?" Ignacio said.

"I been thinkin," the bounty hunter said. "I been thinkin we only got two choices in this life. God or the whiskey. God or the void."

Ignacio nodded.

"That sounds right to me," he said. "Except sometimes I think the two might be the same thing."

"Well," the bounty hunter said, "I don't know anything about that. You see for me, it don't matter who you are. It only matters what you choose. God or the void. God or the nothin."

"How'd you think this ends?" Ignacio said.

"Well, I'm hopin you'll finish your whiskey, put on these here cuffs, and walk out without much fuss," the bounty hunter said.

"I got my pistol," Ignacio said. "I got my carbine and my club."

"I seen that," the bounty hunter said. "And that's the kind a fuss I want to avoid."

"Even if you take me now," Ignacio said. "There'll be a fuss. You know that."

"I know it," the bounty hunter said. "Nothin's perfect."

"Alright then," Ignacio said. "We'll save that for another day."

"That's the spirit," the bounty hunter said. "Will you hand me your guns?"

He took his pistol from his belt and his carbine from the chair next to him and handed them across the table.

"Thank you kindly," the bounty hunter said. "How about that club?"

Ignacio stared him in the eyes.

"Come now," the bounty hunter said. "The club."

"The club?" he said. "You want this club?"

"Don't be that way," the bounty hunter said. "Ain't no need to make a fuss."

"I like a fuss," Ignacio said. "Once in a while."

"That's true enough," the bounty hunter said. "But this ain't once in a while."

"It could be," Ignacio said. "If I want."

"Ain't no such thing as could be," the bounty hunter said. "Only what it is. You know I got my boys out back. So why not just give it here? I'll buy you another whiskey."

"Where you takin me tonight?" Ignacio said.

"Not far," the bounty hunter said. "Know the sheriff a town over. He got a cell waitin for you."

"And we'll hold up there til the rain stops?"

"That's right," the bounty hunter said.

Ignacio thought about that.

"And I got to give you my club?"

"It'd be a nice thing to do," the bounty hunter said. "And then put on these cuffs."

Ignacio looked at him and weighed his options.

"How many boys you say you got out there?" he said.

"I ain't say how many," the bounty hunter said.

"Thought you might," Ignacio said.

"It don't matter," the bounty hunter said. "I got enough. Ain't nothin matter beyond that."

"I suppose that's true," Ignacio said.

He handed the man his club.

"That's a good fellow," the bounty hunter said. "How about these cuffs?"

"How about that whiskey?"

"Alright," the bounty hunter said. "One more. Then we leave."

"One more," Ignacio said. "Just one more."

❧☙

Ignacio and the sheriff stood looking at the dead man. He was slouched up against one of the stable walls and his head was caved in as if crushed by some blunt instrument. The top of his skull was in pieces and the damage was all the more visible because his scalp had been peeled back to the base of his neck. It was pinned down by a thorny wreath which he wore like some ungodly crown, the way a Greek hero might wear his laurel after victory in battle. Dried blood streaked from his head to his neck and down his pale, lifeless body to the ground. His eyes were open wide in terror and Ignacio knew that he had been made to watch everything that had happened to him. His mouth was clenched and twisted, teeth ground together in agony. Over his lawman's uniform was draped a brilliant purple robe. It had gold trim and an ornate gold cross stitched on the center.

"My vestments," Ignacio said.

He had worn them just two weeks before to mark the midpoint of Lent.

38

The sheriff did not answer. He stood with his eyes fixed on the priest, careful to note his every gesture.

Ignacio blessed himself and stared at the corpse. He recognized the dead man as the jailer and hangman from the prison. He had visited Ignacio on more than one occasion to make his confession and ask for the lord's forgiveness. He always confessed the same sins—lacking patience with the inmates, losing his temper with his wife, taking the lord's name in vain, allowing himself to indulge in too much drink. He never sought forgiveness for tying a rope snug round a man's neck and letting that child of god swing from that rope until the weight of his body caused his neck to snap leaving him to hang there limp and cold like a wet towel hung out to dry. It was his job to put those men to death and god asked nothing more than that he do it well. And he did it well.

"You found him this way?" Ignacio said.

"He had a wife and three young boys," the sheriff said.

Ignacio blessed himself again.

"We'll take up a collection," he said.

"Save your collection," the sheriff said and he spat.

Ignacio nodded.

"How'd he end up here?"

"He was on guard last night," the sheriff said. "Some a the prisoners woke to a bang. Santino's cell blown open. Then they saw him come to see what was goin on. Then he was met by two men—Santino and another. He pulls his pistol. The other grabs it by the barrel. He fires straight through the man's hand. Then the man brings a wood club down on his head and drags him out back. Santino just stands there. Not blinkin. Nothin."

"Anyone see what the other looked like?" Ignacio said.

"Too dark to see," the sheriff said. "But they heard

screamin and hollerin. Heard pleadin and beggin and butcherin. And the colts kept kickin and screamin the whole night long."

"It don't make no sense," Ignacio said. "How'd he get my vestments?"

"Thought you might know somethin about that," the sheriff said.

"It don't make no sense," Ignacio said.

"Got a theory a my own," the sheriff said. "Want to guess at what it is?"

"Santino's a loner," Ignacio said. "Ain't got no friend in the world."

"Said he was one a your boys, didn't you, padre?"

"He was," Ignacio said. "It's how I know it. Underneath, he's a good kid. But outside he's hard, selfish, tough to live with. Never known a single soul to like him."

"You like him," the sheriff said.

"I care for him," Ignacio said. "That's a different thing."

"Hate to see him hung, though," the sheriff said. "Wouldn't you?"

"It don't matter what I want," Ignacio said. "It matters what is."

"Ever think you could change what is?" the sheriff said.

"It don't make no sense," Ignacio said. "Santino's a loner."

"What's that got to do with it?" the sheriff said.

"It's got a lot to do with it," Ignacio said. "That boy used to confide in me. Used to tell me he was all alone. Like no one understood him. Not even god. He felt like he'd been left behind. Like even god forgot who he is."

"Lots a people feel that way," the sheriff said.

"Sure," Ignacio said. "But they ain't the types a people who got friends to risk their lives for them.

They ain't the types who got friends to kill for them neither."

"What types a people is?" the sheriff said.

Ignacio scratched his head.

"I don't understand it," he said. "It don't make no sense."

"What's to understand?" the sheriff said. "This man's been murdered. Beat to death with a club. He's been dragged here, scalped, and set to look like your god dressed in a purple robe and crown a thorns. And now you're here and I got you in shackles and I ain't lettin you go. Nothin more to it than that."

"John," Ignacio said.

"Let me see your hands," the sheriff said.

"John," Ignacio said.

"Now," the sheriff said.

Ignacio nodded and held out his hands.

"What's under that kerchief?" the sheriff said.

Ignacio looked at him.

"Go on," the sheriff said. "Take it off."

Ignacio removed the handkerchief from his palm revealing the wound from ma'am's pistol.

"It's what I thought," the sheriff said.

"It's not what it looks like," Ignacio said.

"Never is," the sheriff said and he spat. "Now I'll let you wear them boots back across the hot sand to your cell. But when you get there, you're goin to need to take them off for me."

"Sheriff," Ignacio said. "I told you I don't do that no more."

"I know you did," the sheriff said. "Goin to need you to take them off anyway."

Ignacio nodded and they walked out.

When they got back to the prison, the sheriff led Ignacio into the lone cell in his office. Then he had the priest bend over, pull off his boots, and hand them to him. He took a long knife from his belt, wedged its blade into the heel of the right boot, and popped it off. There was nothing inside. Then he did the same with the left.

"It's what I thought," he said.

Carved into the sole of the shoe was a small, hollow cavity. And stuffed hidden inside were a self-contained pistol cartridge, a wick, and two pieces of flint.

"I forgot about those," Ignacio said. "I've had them boots for years."

"I bet you did," the sheriff said.

"What'll you do with me?" Ignacio said.

"Haven't got that far," the sheriff said. "Keep you in chains for now. Then people'll probably want to see you hanged."

"People wanted to see me hanged before," Ignacio said.

"What's old is new again," the sheriff said.

Ignacio spat.

"Say, tell me," the sheriff said. "Where's that boy Santino?"

"I don't know," Ignacio said.

The sheriff wound up and punched him in the gut.

Ignacio doubled over in pain.

"Where's the boy?" the sheriff said.

"Honest," Ignacio said. "I don't know."

The sheriff wound up and punched him again.

"Where is he?" the sheriff said.

Ignacio sucked at the air.

The sheriff buried his fist in Ignacio's back and the priest fell to the ground.

"Where?" the sheriff said.

Ignacio did not answer.

The sheriff's boot thumped against his ribs.

"How's this goin to be?" he said.

The priest gasped and wheezed.

The sheriff's boot met his face.

"How's this goin to be?" he said.

Ignacio coughed blood.

The sheriff's boot met his face once more.

Ignacio's eyes rolled back in his head and the sheriff kicked him again and again and eventually he went unconscious.

❧

When he awoke, it was dark. He was still in chains and he was on the floor of the cell and a small rat or mouse was chewing on the side of his face. He could see the faint glow of a cigar end burning in the room beyond the bars and he knew that he was being watched. He coughed blood into his cuffed hands and spat on the floor and he tried to straighten himself up.

"How long I been this way?" he said.

"Not long enough," the lawman said.

"Got any water?" he said.

"Yes, sir, I do," the lawman said.

"Could you spare a little?" he said.

The lawman stood and walked over to the cell. He had a canteen of water in his hands. He unscrewed the cap and turned it upside down, pouring the water out on the dirt floor at his feet. The water pattered on the floor and Ignacio coughed and his mouth was dry and sore.

"Well," Ignacio said. "That's a way to be."

"If it were up to me," the lawman said, "there'd be a bullet in your brain right now."

"Glad it ain't up to you," Ignacio said.

"Could be," the lawman said. "If my finger happened to slip on this here trigger."

"No such thing as could be," Ignacio said. "Only what it is."

"That so?" the lawman said.

"That's so," Ignacio said.

The lawman threw his cigar butt through the bars and it bounced off the priest's chest onto the ground. Then he returned to his seat and glared at him through the dark.

"Say let me ask you somethin," Ignacio said.

"Shut up," the lawman said.

"If whoever clubbed your friend there clubbed him outside a Santino's cell and if Santino went with him willingly, why's there blood on the walls inside?"

"Shut up," the lawman said.

"You saw it," Ignacio said. "Sheriff tasted it with his tongue. How'd that blood get there?"

"This is the last time I'm goin to tell you," the lawman said. "Shut. Up."

"You think whoever clubbed your friend forced Santino to go with him?" Ignacio said. "Like against his will?"

"That's it," the lawman said.

He got up, unlocked the door, entered the cell, and punched Ignacio square in the jaw.

Ignacio fell to the floor. He coughed and spat blood.

Then the lawman exited the cell, closed the door, and returned to his seat.

Ignacio did not say another word. But he noticed that when the lawman had entered, he had not pulled the door of the cell shut behind him. He thought about that as he sat alone in the darkness and wondered what would happen next.

TUESDAY OF HOLY WEEK ✺

E arly the next morning, when the altar boy
descended the bell tower stairs, he was met by
a beautiful young woman with ruddy cheeks.
The girl had curly, strawberry hair, pale white skin,
and dark purple bruises on her face and neck. She
wore a simple blue dress and had a white scarf
wrapped around her head. Her eyes were somber, her
demeanor pensive. She looked as though she hadn't
slept, as if she'd been up brooding over something
all night. The boy felt uncomfortable and he wished
she would go. Instead, she waited at the bottom of
the stairs and forced a smile as he approached.

"Know where he is?" Maryellen said.

The boy shrugged.

"Have you seen him this mornin?"

He shook his head.

"No," she said. "Didn't think so."

He looked down.

"I'm worried," Maryellen said. "Had these awful
dreams. Couldn't sleep a wink. And now he ain't here.
That's no good."

The boy coughed into his sleeve.

"He's normally here," she said.

The boy nodded.

"Where else could he be?"

The two stood in silence and listened to the wind
blow against the outside of the church. A couple
of parishioners entered, crossing themselves, and
genuflecting before the altar. She looked over at the
wooden crucifix and let out a sigh. One of the churchgoers gave her a look but she did not seem to notice.

"Ever dream you're fallin?" she said. "Like you keep
fallin and fallin and there's no one there to catch
you?"

The boy nodded.

"How do you wake from a dream like that?" she said. "Can't pull yourself from a dream like that. No matter how hard you try."

The boy thought about that.

"When was the last time you seen him?"

The boy shrugged.

"Yesterday mornin?"

He nodded.

"Okay," she said. "I best be goin."

She walked to the door and opened it. The morning sun broke in white and hot and she shielded her eyes with her hand. Then she left and the door shut behind her.

"What's a girl like that doin in a place like this?" someone asked.

The boy shrugged.

"Ain't no place for a girl like that."

He walked away.

When he entered the sacristy, he noticed that the door to the back closet was ajar. It looked as if someone had busted the lock and rummaged through. He didn't know what to make of that so he closed the door and went on with his morning routine. He didn't expect to see Father Ignacio but still he prepared for mass as if it was an ordinary day. He even laid out the priest's vestments.

"Where is he?"

The altar boy looked up with surprise.

Standing in the doorway was a pale, stocky man with black hair and yellow eyes, the man who'd come to the church to visit Ignacio the night before. He smiled a crooked smile and used his dirty, bandaged hand to smooth his black hair.

The altar boy looked at him.

"Asked you a question," the man said. "Best be answerin."

46

"You ain't supposed to be back here," the boy said.

"Where's your priest?" the man said.

"I don't know," the boy said.

"You expectin him?" the man said.

"I don't know," the boy said.

"You one a his orphan boys?" the man said.

The boy nodded.

"What happened to your ma and your pa?"

The boy looked at the ground.

"Ain't they want you? Ain't they love you no more?"

The boy did not answer.

"It don't matter," the man said. "You could come live with me."

The boy was nervous.

"Always wanted to get myself a son. You'd do jus fine. Even let you call me pa."

The boy's mouth felt dry. He coughed a dry cough.

"Go on," the man said. "Call me pa."

The boy did not answer.

"Okay," the man said. "Okay."

He turned as if he was going to leave. But then he turned back.

"Say, let me ask you somethin," he said. "You ever want to do somethin bad?"

The boy looked up.

"You ever want to make a mess a things?"

The boy looked at him intently.

"I been thinkin," the man said. "Thinkin how nice it might be to do a lot a bad things."

"What kind a things?" the boys said.

"Bad things," the man said. "Real bad."

"How come?" the boy said.

"No reason," the man said. "Jus to do em. Jus cause I can."

"I don't know," the boy said.

"Oh no?" the man said. "Let me try again. You ever want a prove how bad you is?"

"What'd you mean?" the boy said.

"You know," the man said. "How rotten you can be? Prove you ain't no better than a wolf or some other scavengin beast?"

The boy shrugged.

"You ever want a prove he made a mistake? That all he done was one big mistake?"

"Who?" the boy said.

The man nodded his head toward a gold crucifix that stood on the tabernacle where they kept the uneaten hosts.

"Who else?"

"I don't know," the boy said.

"Sure you do," the man said. "You know just what I'm after. You feel it too."

"I don't know," the boy said.

"Think about it," the man said. "In your heart you know he never should a made you. You know you ain't worth the clay. All I'm askin is, ain't you never wanted to prove it? Ain't you never wanted to make him see what you see?"

There was a commotion outside and the boy looked past the man into the church. The few churchgoers got up from their pews and walked out to see what was the matter. Then he heard panic. Then shouting. Then screams.

He looked at the man.

"Who are you?" he said.

"Your priest," the man said, "I'd like to talk to him. Be a good boy and let him know I was here."

The boy exited the sacristy leaving the man standing alone in the doorway. He walked across the church to the door. When he opened it, the white sun blinded him and he rubbed his eyes with his hands. After a moment, he regained his vision and saw a crowd of people hollering and shouting and shoving one another. He pushed his way through the crowd until he came to what the noise was all about. Then he felt a queasy feeling in the bottom of his stomach and he thought he might faint. He took a few deep breaths and backed away. Then he did faint. His eyes rolled back in his head and he lost control of his limbs. He stumbled and fell to the clay earth. But no one saw him fall. Their focus was on the man lying dead at their feet.

❦

Ignacio awoke in his cell with a start. He looked around the office and tried to remember where he was. It was the first morning in over half a decade that he began without saying mass. The chains on his wrists and ankles were tight and they rubbed against his bare skin causing it to scab and bleed. His mouth tasted metallic like blood. His head ached. Each time he inhaled, a sharp pain shot through his chest and he cringed and held his ribs. He coughed and it hurt to cough and tears welled in his eyes. He looked up at the lawman who watched him struggle and he spat some blood on the floor.

"Water?" he said.

"Fuck yourself," the lawman said.

He nodded.

"Thought so."

He grabbed hold of the bars of his cell and pulled himself to his feet. His back cracked as he stood and he straightened himself up. Then he turned and faced the small cot on which he had slept. He knelt down beside it and began to pray. He used the links of his chains to count his prayers.

"Ave Maria, gratia plena, Dominus tecum."

"Shut up," the lawman said.

"Sancta Maria, Mater Dei, ora pro nobis peccatoribus."

"Shut up," the lawman said.

"Gloria Patri, et Filio, et Spiritui Sancto, sicut erat in principio, et nunc, et semper, et in saecula saeculorum."

"You shut up with that goddamn voodoo," the lawman said.

He rose to his feet and approached the cell.

Then the door to the office swung open and in walked the sheriff.

"We got another one," he said.

"Another what?" the lawman said.

"Grab your rifle and come with me," the sheriff said.

The two hurried out, leaving Ignacio to pray.

❧❦☙

The last time Ignacio had been imprisoned was a rain-soaked night in the summer of 1850 when he sat awake in a Texas prison cell waiting for the jailer to fall asleep. He had been left there by a fellow bountyman who was fixing to collect a bounty on his head. Where that bountyman was, he did not know. But he planned to find out and he was going to do everything in his power to make sure he never got that money.

He shared a cell with a wiry-looking teen, short, black, scrappy, with a patchy beard, and dark brown eyes. His fellow inmate was tapping his hand on his knee and singing in a twangy voice about being a drunken-hearted man and about how sin and drunkenness was the cause of it all.

"Hey, that ain't half bad," Ignacio said.

"Thank you kindly."

"What's your name?" Ignacio said.

"I ain't got none."

"How's that?" Ignacio said.

"I ain't got none cause I ain't got no one to give it."

"No parents?"

"No, sir."

50

"No family?"

"Ain't even know what that mean."

"Where you from?"

"Here and there," the inmate said. "Back east I's work in the fields. Born in chains. Fixin to die in chains too. But since I run off, I lived pretty much everywhere."

"You a runaway?" Ignacio said.

"Yes, sir," the inmate said. "Got a three hundred dolla tag on this mug."

"That much?" Ignacio said.

The inmate smiled.

"I done some things."

"What you in for?"

"You got eyes."

"Well," Ignacio said. "I mean besides that."

"I kill a man."

"A white man?"

"What else?"

"That is trouble," Ignacio said.

"It sure is."

"How'd it happen?"

"With a knife."

"Tough way to go," Ignacio said.

"That sumbitch got jus what he deserve," the inmate said.

"How'd it happen?"

"You want to know my story?"

Ignacio nodded. "Yes, I do."

"Well, it's like this," the inmate said. "I was at this busted up whore house not far from here. Pickin a real nice one for myself too, little ugly girl with nub toes. Been a while and my blood was gettin hot. We was jus about to head up stairs when this old boy walks in and says, 'No negroes.' 'I ain't no negroes,' I says. 'I's one negro. And I come for a reason.' 'Take it elsewheres,' he says, 'before we have a row.' 'A row's what I come for,' I says, 'so let me go and have it.' That's when he pulls out this big sucker, look like a banker's special, and points that barrel right at my chest. 'I'll let you have it,' he says, 'if you don't go on and get.' Well, I don't like havin a gun pulled on me. Never have. Don't like what it suggests."

"Didn't expect you would," Ignacio said.

"So I wait out back by an old, rotted log. Wait by the jakes. Figure sooner or later this bald bastard's goin to have to come down and drain it out."

"Did he?"

"You know he did. About a half an hour goes by and here's old boy strollin on down with no shirt and his belt undid and a Sunday smile from ear to ear."

"What'd you do?"

"Stick him with my long knife. What else? Get him right there between the ribs. Now he's bleedin and gaspin and lookin at me all sad like. And I bend down and pull my knife out and wipe it on my shirt and I say 'How's that for a row?' Then I walk back up from the jakes, go in, and have myself a time."

"Well, there's your mistake," Ignacio said. "Shouldn't a gone back in."

"Yes, sir," the inmate said. "There it is."

"They goin to hang you?"

"Bet they might."

"You want to live?"

"Yes, sir," the inmate said. "I surely do."

Ignacio nodded. "I might be able to help you with that."

"I'd appreciate it," the inmate said. "I would."

Ignacio nodded.

The two sat in the silence of the cell listening to the rain beat down.

"Say," the inmate said. "Can I maybe tell you somethin?"

"That depends," Ignacio said.

"Nothin bad," the inmate said. "Jus something I ain't never tell nobody."

"Why'd you want to tell me a thing like that?"

"Don't know," the inmate said. "Everybody gots to have somebody."

"I ain't your confessor," Ignacio said.

"I ain't askin you to be. But maybe jus tonight."

"I ain't your priest."

"No," the inmate said. "But you's my friend."

Ignacio nodded. "I guess I am."

"You ever love somebody?" the inmate said.

"Now we're talkin about me?" Ignacio said.

"I loves somebody," the inmate said. "A girl."

"I hope so," Ignacio said.

"Ain't even know her name."

"It can happen."

"She dead now."

"That can happen too."

"Want to see somethin?" the inmate said.

"That depends," Ignacio said.

The inmate bent over and pulled off his boot. He shook it and a small, black object rolled out into his palm. It was dark in the cell and hard to see. He held it up, pressed it to his mouth, and gave it a kiss.

"What you got there?" Ignacio said.

"Her little toe," the inmate said.

"How's that?" Ignacio said.

"Her toe," the inmate said. "I gots her little toe."

❧

Ignacio had just completed his third rosary when the door to the sheriff's office swung open. He pulled himself up onto his cot and turned to face his guest. It was the sheriff and he had a mean look on his face. His brow was tense and wrinkled. His eyes were like eyes that had seen too much. They fixed themselves on their prisoner and waited for him to speak. He coughed and held his ribs. The sheriff cleared his throat and spat and Ignacio spat and his spittle was full of dry blood.

"How'd you do it?" the sheriff said.

"Could I get some water?" Ignacio said.

"Who you got helpin you?" the sheriff said.

"Real thirsty," Ignacio said. "Ain't had a sip a nothin all night."

"Best start talkin," the sheriff said. "Things ain't shapin up for you."

"John," Ignacio said. "I need somethin to drink. I can't go much longer."

The sheriff walked to his desk and pulled a bottle of whiskey from his top drawer. He poured it into a small, metal cup. It splashed in the cup and some dribbled down the side. Then he walked to the cell and handed it through the bars. Ignacio took it and drank it down and he coughed as he drank.

"Good?" the sheriff said.

Ignacio nodded.

"More?"

Ignacio nodded again.

The sheriff took the cup, filled it, and passed it back through the bars.

Ignacio drank it down greedily and he sighed when he was done.

"Say," the sheriff said. "You remember that negro fella? The one from all them years back."

Ignacio looked at him intently.

"The one you was with in Texas," the sheriff said.

"I remember," Ignacio said.

"Young boy," the sheriff said. "A runaway."

"I remember," Ignacio said.

"I ever tell you what happened to him?" the sheriff said.

Ignacio coughed.

"After the three a us parted ways?" the sheriff said. "I tell you how it all turned out?"

"You did," Ignacio said.

"I ever tell you about Mississippi?"

"Yes," Ignacio said.

"About what happened when we got there?"

"You told," Ignacio said.

"You ever think about that?"

"I do," Ignacio said.

"It ever bother you?"

"It does," Ignacio said.

"It ever keep you up at night?"

"Yes," Ignacio said.

"That's good," the sheriff said. "I'm glad to hear it."

Ignacio spat.

"How'd you like it if that was you?" the sheriff said.

Ignacio glared at him.

"How'd you feel if you ended up that way?"

"Might be for the best," Ignacio said. "It's what I deserve."

"Oh, I don't think you believe that," the sheriff said. "But I'll tell you what. If I don't get some answers and get them quick, we're goin to find out."

꽃

The third of the murders was more gruesome than the previous two. The victim had been beaten, tortured, whipped, and scalped. He had been dressed up in a brown tunic and made to wear a wreath of jagged thorns wrapped tight around his skull. He had been taken to the outskirts of town where he had had an oversized tree trunk fastened to his back with chains. Then he had been forced to march barefoot across the hot desert sand, dragging the trunk as far as he could go. He made it more than a mile before collapsing under the weight of the wood in front of the old Spanish church. The bells of church rang out above and a crowd of people gathered to bear witness to the scene. No one offered to help. They watched in terror as the man slowly suffocated in the sand at their feet. The wood pressed down into his back and his lungs collapsed and he was crushed. He gasped and gasped until he could gasp no more. Then he let out one final, pitiful cry and died.

Panic spread through the crowd and no one knew what to do. There were women weeping and beating their breasts. There were men walking about asking what was the matter. There were people vomiting uncontrollably and others crying and screaming and pulling at their hair. There was weeping and wailing and gnashing of teeth and the altar boy had fainted no more than a few feet away. He lay there unconscious and unnoticed on the hot desert earth. The sun beat down on his face and it burnt his cheeks but he did not wake and no one saw him lying there. Then the sheriff arrived on horseback and the lawman was at his side. He looked at the scene and spat and calmed his horse. Then he fired his rifle into air to get the crowd's attention. When everyone was quiet, he assured them that there was nothing to worry about. The murderer, he said, was in custody. As much as it pained him to tell it, the beloved Father Ignacio de la Cruz was responsible for this man's death. More than that, he was responsible for the deaths of two others. An orphan and an officer of the law. But now he was locked up in a prison cell with chains on hands and chains on feet and there was no need to worry. He would be strung up before the week was through and life would go back to normal.

"When'd you take him in?" one of the townspeople said.

"Yesterday mornin," the lawman said.

"Then how's he done this?"

A murmur rose up in the crowd and the sheriff gave the lawman a straight look.

"Now, now," the sheriff said. "Ain't no need to worry. The murderer's in shackles back at the county jail. He'll get his soon enough."

"Ain't no murderer!" someone called out. "It was injuns!"

"Apache!" another yelled. "Savages!"

"No," someone said. "This here's the work of a damned Mexican!"

"Now, now," the sheriff said. "No need to cause a fuss."

"Maybe there's two murderers!" a woman shouted.

"Or three," another cried.

"What about the children?" someone said. "Who'll protect our children?"

"We ain't safe," a man said. "Look at this boy. Butchered him like a pig."

The sheriff fired his rifle once more and a hush came over the crowd.

"You listen," he said. "I'm the sheriff a this god-damn town and if I say it's safe, it's safe. Now we need y'all to clear up out a here. Get on home and don't you worry another wink. We got everythin under control. Got our best men on the job."

The lawman nodded and spat.

"We need a posse!" someone said.

"We ain't need no such thing," the sheriff said. "Now get!"

The crowd dispersed in every direction and the people talked among themselves about what they had witnessed and what ought to be done. When they had cleared out, the sheriff noticed the altar boy. He dismounted his horse, walked over, and slapped the boy straight across the face. The boy came to and looked at him with confusion.

"You get the hell out a here," the sheriff said.

The boy jumped to his feet and ran off.

"What you make of it?" the lawman said.

"Is it who I think it is?" the sheriff said.

"Yes sir," the lawman said. "That's him if I ever seen him."

The sheriff walked over and bent down by the corpse.

"It don't make no sense," he said.

"What don't?" the lawman said.

"What's he doin here?" the sheriff said.

"Looks dead to me," the lawman said.

"Don't be smart," the sheriff said. "How'd he get that way?"

"The priest," the lawman said. "How else?"

"No," the sheriff said. "Can't be."

"Could be," the lawman said. "What if he set him like that before we took him in?"

"No," the sheriff said. "That don't work. These wounds is fresh. This boy's been scalped this mornin."

"You ain't thinkin apache?" the lawman said.

"I ain't thinkin nothin," the sheriff said. "That's the problem."

"Well, if the priest ain't bust him out a that cell then who?"

"I don't know," the sheriff said. "I surely don't."

"I saw him," the lawman said. "Passin somethin through them bars. Had to be somethin to do with this whole mess."

The sheriff grunted.

"Help me turn him over," he said.

They dug their hands into the sand beneath the corpse and turned it over onto the wood. When they did, a pocket of air exhaled from its lungs and blood gargled in its throat and bubbled from its mouth.

The lawman jumped.

"He's alive," he said.

"No," the sheriff said. "He ain't."

The lawman kicked the corpse with his boot.

It didn't move.

"Poor bastard," the lawman said.

The sheriff grunted.

"How could someone do somethin like this?" the lawman said.

"It's what I'm tryin to figure out."

"There are some things I'll never understand," the lawman said.

"You have to," the sheriff said. "If you can't understand it, you won't solve the case."

"How'd you mean?"

"I mean that to do this job, you gotta be part criminal. At least in your mind. And that's the worse offense."

"I don't follow," the lawman said.

"I know you don't," the sheriff said and he let out a sigh. "I'm glad you don't."

The two stood in silence. The sheriff swatted at something on his neck. Then he turned and faced the old church. He had never taken the time to really look at it. But now he felt that there was something oddly beautiful about it. Something he could not name.

A black crow perched itself at the top of the bell tower and it let out a hideous cry.

"What's it mean?" the sheriff said to himself. "What's all this mean?"

"Say," the lawman said. "What's that hangin round his neck?"

A pair of wooden beads dangled from the dead man's throat.

"Look like a rosary to me."

"What's a rosary?" the lawman said.

"Use it to pray," the sheriff said.

"He ain't prayin no more," the lawman said.

"Maybe more than ever," the sheriff said.

"What good's it do him now?"

"Don't know," the sheriff said. "It's what they call a mystery."

"I don't like it," the lawman said. "You gettin all voodoo on me."

"No," the sheriff said. "I'm jus gettin old."

"You findin faith in old age?" the lawman said.

"No," the sheriff said. "I'm losin it."

✦✦✦

They returned to the prison, entered Ignacio's cell, and beat him until he bled. The sheriff hit him in the ribs and the lawman grabbed him by his chains, stood him up straight, and punched him in the jaw. He fell back against the wall and then slouched over to the floor. He coughed and began to vomit. There was nothing in his stomach but whiskey and bile so he heaved and sucked at the air. The sheriff gave him a halfhearted kick. The lawman put his foot on his face and pressed it into the dirt. Ignacio breathed in and dirt and shit filled his nose and mouth. But he did not cry out.

"What you know about that boy Santino?" the sheriff said.

Ignacio gasped.

"Stand him up," the sheriff said. "Up."

The lawman stood him up.

"Look at me," the sheriff said. "Look in my eye."

Ignacio's face was swollen and bruised. He peered out through dark, swollen slits.

"Talk," the sheriff said.

"Tell me what you want me to say," Ignacio said. "And I'll say it."

"Don't play games," the sheriff said. "This ain't goin to end well for you."

Ignacio spat.

"Can't get much worse."

"Believe you me," the sheriff said. "It can."

The lawman punched Ignacio in the gut.

Ignacio smiled and spat.

"You can do better," he said.

The lawman grabbed him by his ears and banged his face against the bars.

"Alright," the sheriff said. "This ain't no dick swingin contest. Go fetch us a bucket a water."

"But sheriff," the lawman said.

"Water," the sheriff said. "Now."

The lawman turned and walked out.

Ignacio pulled himself to his feet. He and the sheriff stood in silence, each staring at the other.

"You got somethin to tell me?" the sheriff said.

Ignacio did not answer.

"You realize," the sheriff said, "I got the power to let you go and the power to see you hanged?"

Ignacio spat.

The lawman returned with a bucket of water. It was cool and clear. The sheriff dipped his hands and washed off the blood. He gave the bucket to Ignacio and let him do the same. Ignacio cupped his hands and filled them with water. He raised them to his face and let the water bead over his raw skin. It was cool and clear and it glimmered and dribbled down his face. He let out a long sigh. Then he dipped his hands in once more and raised them to his lips. He drank and coughed and drank and spat.

"Good?" the sheriff said.

"Good," Ignacio said.

"Good," the sheriff said. "You'll be strung up tomorrow at first light. That ought to cool some tensions while we sort all this out."

Ignacio poured the bucket over his head and let the water wash over his frail and aching body. He sighed and watched the sheriff walk out.

"Look like it's jus you and me tonight, padre," the lawman said.

Ignacio grunted.

"Any last requests? You want me to get the local priest to hear your confession?"

Ignacio knelt down and began to pray.

The lawman locked the cell and walked to the sheriff's desk. He sat there and fixed his eyes on his prisoner. He watched him. Listened. Then he got up and paced around the office. He walked back and forth, stopped at the desk, straightened some papers, walked to the window, looked out at the late-afternoon sun. In the distance he saw a lone coyote skulk past. There was something hanging from its mouth. Something cold and lifeless. He walked over to the bars and stood there. He did not say or think anything. He just stood and stared. He watched the priest—hands clasped tight, head bowed low, body bruised and bleeding.

"Can I ask you somethin?"

Ignacio continued to pray.

"Can I tell you somethin?"

Ignacio looked up.

"My wife," the lawman said. "When she lost the second one."

Ignacio looked him in the eyes.

The lawman looked away.

"Well," he said. "I wasn't too good."

"How'd you mean?"

"Well," he said. "I was tough. I did some things. Some things I can't undo."

Ignacio studied his face.

"Blamed her I guess. Let her know it."

Ignacio sat up on his cot.

"Did some things I shouldn't a done."

"When did it happen?" Ignacio said.

The lawman gave him a look.

There was a pause.

"You regret it?" Ignacio said.

The lawman looked at the floor.

"You ever tell her?" Ignacio said.

The lawman shook his head.

"What's the use?" he said. "No goin back now."

"There's forgiveness in this world," Ignacio said. "If you want it."

The lawman looked at him.

"No," he said. "What's done is done."

Ignacio nodded.

"That's true," he said. "It can't be taken back. But it can be named. You can bear witness."

"It's too late," the lawman said. "Too late for all that now."

"It's never too late," Ignacio said.

He rose to his feet and walked to the bars.

"We can't change our sins but we can own them. And there can be healin in that."

The lawman recoiled.

"Fuck you," he said. "What you know about it?"

"I know about forgiveness," Ignacio said.

"Fuck your forgiveness," the lawman said.

"Ain't my forgiveness I'm talkin about," Ignacio said.

"Fuck you," the lawman said. "Fuck your god too."

Ignacio nodded. "I can understand that."

"Understand this," the lawman said. "Tomorrow mornin, when they string you up, it's goin to be the happiest I been in years."

"I believe that," Ignacio said.

"Believe it," the lawman said. "If I could, I'd watch you die over and over. Each and every day until my last."

Ignacio nodded. "I can understand that too."

"The only thing that'd make me happier," the lawman said, "is to do it myself."

He looked at the priest with hate in his eyes.

"Well," Ignacio said. "What's stoppin you?"

The lawman walked over to the cell door.

"You said it yourself," Ignacio said. "Just you and me here tonight."

The lawman opened the door and stepped in.

"We'll talk more about forgiveness later," Ignacio said.

He dropped his shoulder, rushed at the lawman, and tackled him into the bars. The lawman's fist came down hard on his skull and Ignacio yelled out in pain. But he did not stop fighting. He took the lawman to the floor and the two wrestled in the dirt. The lawman wrapped his hands around Ignacio's throat and squeezed. Ignacio was bleeding and his blood squirted on the lawman's face. The lawman licked it with his tongue and grunted and he smiled an awful smile. Ignacio gasped for air and he felt the life leaving his body. He flailed and swung his chains wildly in desperation. They cracked the lawman on the side of the head and he doubled over in pain. Ignacio got up and hit him again and again until he was unconscious. Then he took the ring of keys from the lawman's belt, freed himself from the chains, and used them to fasten the lawman to the bars. He grabbed his boots and the lawman's pistol from the desk and limped out into the redness of the evening sun.

WEDNESDAY OF HOLY WEEK

She held a pistol in one hand, a rosary in the other, and she laid awake thinking about Ignacio, what he had said before leaving her that night, and what was going to happen when the sun came up. He had ridden in on horseback, slumped over the neck of a handsome gray colt. The horse was the sheriff's. He had stolen it from the stable and set the others free. He had hoped to put some distance between himself and the law but knew they would not be far behind.

When he got to ma'am's, he hid the horse behind the bushes out back. Then he pulled himself in through an open window and dragged himself upstairs trying hard not to attract attention. He tapped on her door with three gentle taps. When she answered, she found him standing there, bleeding from his face and mouth. There was dirt in his hair and dry blood on his clothes. There were bruises around his eyes and scratches on his hands and neck. His face was swollen and raw. The heels of his boots had been cut off. The bare bottoms of his feet stuck to the wood floor.

"What in the hell is this?" said a toothless man from inside the room.

Ignacio pointed a pistol at him.

"Get out," he said.

The man looked at him intently.

Ignacio cocked the hammer.

"I ain't sayin it twice."

The man rose from the bed, pulled on a pair of overalls, and walked out cussing.

"Father," Maryellen said.

She reached up and touched his cheek.

He pulled away.

"You remember what I gave you?" he said.

"Come in," she said. "Sit down."

He entered and she closed the door behind him.

"You remember what I asked you to keep?"

"Sit," she said. "You ain't well."

He stumbled to the edge of the bed and sat.

"Where is it?" he said.

"What happened to you?"

He coughed.

"Where?" he said. "I need it."

She sat down next to him.

"You're shakin," she said.

"I need it," he said. "I need it."

"Hush," she said. "Lay back."

He laid back.

"I need it," he said.

"Hush," she said. "Close your eyes."

He closed his eyes.

She pulled the blankets up over him.

"You remember?" he said. "When I first came here."

"I remember," she said.

She rubbed his brow and began to sing.

> *Qué linda manito que tengo yo,*
> *Qué linda y blanquita que Dios me dio.*
> *Qué lindos ojitos que tengo yo,*
> *Qué lindos y negritos que Dios me dio.*

It was a song she had learned as a child. She couldn't speak but broken Spanish, yet she knew every word. She looked down at Ignacio and wondered what it meant. Something sad, she thought. Beautiful and sad.

> *Qué linda boquita que tengo yo,*
> *Qué linda y rojita que Dios me dio.*
> *Qué lindas patitas que tengo yo,*
> *Qué lindas y gorditas que Dios me dio.*

Ignacio shivered and his teeth chattered in his mouth. She cradled him and rocked him and sang until he fell asleep. Then she hummed softly and stroked his hair.

A short while later, he awoke with a start. He looked nervously around the room.

"Hush," she said. "Hush."

She took a damp cloth from a bucket and dabbed his face. She opened his shirt and wiped the blood from his chest.

He looked at her intently.

"These scars," she said. "Where'd you get these scars?"

"I need it," he said.

"You told me about that one on your face. That you got it as a boy. But I ain't know nothin about these scars."

His torso was covered with thick purple scars, raised and knobbled like rope.

He pushed her hands away and buttoned his shirt.

"Where is it?" he said.

"You said you'd never ask for it."

"Never's a long time."

She looked at him with sadness in her eyes.

"This has to do with them dead boys," she said.

"It has to do with the one who's been killin em," he said.

"I don't like this," she said.

"I don't like it neither," he said. "But it ain't about what we like."

"What then?" she said.

"Where is it?" he said.

She pointed at the floorboards.

He sat up and pulled himself out of bed with a grunt.

She came to his aid.

"I'm okay," he said. "I'm alright."

He limped over, bent down, and lifted the wooden boards.

"I don't like this," she said.

He reached into the hollow and pulled out an old cotton sack. It was moth-bitten and covered with dust. Stitched on the side was a patch that read *8th Rifle Company: Texas*.

"I don't like this," she said.

He opened it.

Inside was a Colt Model 1848 percussion revolver, a Hall-North .52 caliber carbine rifle, a worn pair of cowhide boots, an apache scalping knife, and a knotted wooden club.

"I don't like this," she said.

He loaded the guns, put the Colt in his belt, slung the rifle over his shoulder, kicked on the boots, and stood.

"Here," he said and he handed her the lawman's pistol.

"No," she said.

"Take it," he said. "I got somethin I need you to do."

"No," she said. "I ain't goin to use it."

He looked her in her eyes.

She looked away.

He took her hand in his.

She looked down.

He lifted her chin. Then he opened her palm and put the pistol in her hand.

"Take this," he said. "For me."

"Okay," she said. "Okay."

"I'm leavin town," he said. "But I'll be back."

"Where you goin?" she said.

"To the hills," he said.

"What's in the hills?" she said.

"Got someone to see," he said.

She shuddered.

"It's the only way," he said.

"What's he goin to tell you that you ain't already know?"

"If I knew that," he said, "I wouldn't be goin."

"That man's a devil," she said.

"Sometimes the devil's the only one you can trust."

"I don't trust him," she said.

"It's the only way," he said.

"What you expectin to find?" she said. "What's he goin to show you that your own eyes can't?"

"Whatever's goin on," he said, "it ain't like everythin else. It's evil. I mean the real thing. I can't understand it. Can't even begin to. That man in them hills, he alone knows what all this means."

"No," she said. "There ain't no understandin evil. And you can't cast out devils with devils."

"Well," he said. "We'll find out."

She looked at the floor.

"What you need me to do?" she said.

"The orphans," he said. "They ain't safe."

She nodded.

"Most of them's leavin town tomorrow," he said. "Goin to celebrate the Triduum at the Mission in Tucson. But little Bernardo, my altar boy, he's stayin here. Supposed to help me this whole week."

"I saw him," she said. "This mornin."

"How's he doin?" he said.

"Scared," she said. "Missin you."

"You got to protect that boy," he said. "You can't let nothin happen to that boy."

"What you need me to do?" she said.

"Go to the church at sunup," he said. "Find him, bring him here, keep him hidden, keep him safe."

"Okay," she said.

"Okay," he said.

She looked at the floor.

"I best be goin," he said.

69

"Wait," she said.

"What?" he said.

"Kiss me," she said.

He leaned in and kissed her cheek.

"No," she said. "Kiss me."

"When I get back," he said.

"You'll come back?" she said.

"I'll come back," he said and he grabbed his guns and club and walked out.

Maryellen spent the rest of the night staring at the ceiling, replaying their conversation in her head. She held a pistol in one hand, a rosary in the other, and she prayed and waited for the morning to come. Then she got up and walked to the window. The moon outside was full and bright, the dull glow of the pale sun just visible on the horizon. There was dry thunder rumbling in the distance and every so often she saw a flash of sterile light. The wind rustled the dry grass and she listened to the sound of the cicada. She waited and listened. Then she cocked the hammer of the pistol, concealed it in her dress, and left for the church without knowing what she was going to find.

❧❧❧

Brother Markel the Seer lived in the hills just west of town. He had been there for decades fasting and praying and mortifying his flesh. Over the years, he had become a part of the town's folklore. Some said he was divinely inspired. They called him a mystic, a prophet, a holy fool. Others said he was possessed. They claimed he practiced black magic, drank the blood of animals, and sacrificed to demons. There were stories about him abducting children, stealing their eyes, and feeding them to his offspring, little beakfaced gremlins who lived on the moon. People warned not to go too close to the hills at night. They said you could hear screams like the wailing of the damned. They said that the old monk had found a secret passway into hell and that he descended down and made sure there would be no second harrow.

His defenders rejected such claims. They attributed to him countless miracles. They said he had cured a man of typhoid with his shadow and freed another from epilepsies with the spittle from his tongue. They said he survived on nothing but locusts and berries and the roots of wild plants. They said he fasted continuously, sometimes for months on end, and that he only broke his rule to consume the holy eucharist and to drink the blood of his god.

"He learnt at the knee of Beelzebub."

"He has the faith to do mighty deeds."

"He's a wolf lurkin in sheep's clothin."

"He's a tree known by its fruits."

Few people had ever seen him. But even those who had were unclear on what they had seen. Some swore he was a monster, his face twisted like a strange satyr's mask from some festival gone by. Others said he was unbearably beautiful—with eyes like an angel of god. Everyone knew who he was but no one knew what to believe. They feared him and avoided him and begged for his prayers. A group of elderly women gathered each week to leave offerings on a large, flat stone at the foot of one of the hills. They left bread and wine and notes on which they had written their intentions. And each week when they returned they found that their gifts had been taken. They were certain that Brother Markel watched over them and delivered their prayers straight to heaven.

Ignacio had met Markel once, nearly six years before, prior to becoming a priest. He had traveled to the hills at night and knelt to pray. When he finished, he found that he was not alone. A man stood behind him in the dark. Ignacio rose and turned to face him.

The man was short, shabby, frighteningly thin. His shirt was made of sackcloth and he had thick iron chains wrapped tight around his waist. He held a pilgrim's staff in one hand and a wooden rosary in the other. He was barefoot with cracked brown toes and dirty black feet. His teeth were small and sharp like the teeth of an animal. His face reminded Ignacio of the lepers he had seen in Louisiana. It was covered with sores and lesions, gray scales and brown spots. His eyes were blue like water. They were beautiful but useless. The man stared off in obscure directions. He was utterly blind.

"Ya've come to make yer confession."

The man seemed to whistle when he spoke.

"I've come to pray," Ignacio said.

"Ya've got much to atone fer."

"Who are you?"

"Shhh!" Markel hissed. "Listen. Yer brother's blood cries out from the soil."

The emaciated man bent down and pressed his ear to the earth.

Ignacio looked at him intently.

The man rose to his knees and began praying in a strange tongue. He raised his arms to the heavens and shouted something inaudible. Then he picked up a stick and used it to write in the dirt.

Ignacio studied him, not sure of what to do. He walked over and read what the monk had written. It was a list of names. The names of all of the men Ignacio had killed.

"Who are you?" Ignacio said.

"Repent of yer sins and turn to god," Markel said. "The kingdom is at hand."

He scratched one final name onto the bottom of the list.

Ignacio bent down to read it.

Ignacio de la Cruz.

He ran his hand over the dirt to erase the name and when he looked up again, the monk was gone.

❧

The rain continued to beat down on the Texas prison on a summer night in 1850. It pinged off the tin roof like hail and poured in through the barred windows. The two prisoners sat in silence. The inmate looked about anxiously. He rubbed his hands together and cleared his throat. Then he got up and paced about the cell. The other prisoner, Ignacio, sat motionless in the dark.

"How's we goin to do it?" the inmate whispered.

"Shut it," Ignacio said. "Don't you make me regret tellin."

"Okay," the inmate said. "Sorry."

He sat back down.

"Can I maybe tell you somethin?" the inmate said.

"Ain't you know no more songs?" Ignacio said.

"I know lots a songs," the inmate said.

"Well," Ignacio said.

"What kind a songs you lookin to hear?"

"I don't know," Ignacio said. "Somethin you learnt in the fields."

"I ain't know no gospel."

"I ain't askin for gospel."

"Okay," the inmate said. "How about this one right here?"

He began clapping his hands and singing in a twangy voice.

> *I went to town the other day*
> *Lookin to get myself a lay.*
> *Instead this preacher come up to me*
> *Says boy your god from Galilee*
> *Know all your sins and whatya done*
> *So I smack him in the mouth an say,*
> *He know that one.*

73

Ignacio laughed.

"You got a good voice," he said.

"Thank you kindly," the inmate said.

"Where'd you learn to sing like that?"

"Been singin my whole life," the inmate said. "Don't know no other way."

"Well it's good," Ignacio said. "You done good."

"Say, let me ask you," the boy said. "You ever have any regrets?"

"Sure," Ignacio said. "A man with no regrets is a man who don't know himself."

"That right?" the inmate said.

"I say it is," Ignacio said.

"I got regrets," the inmate said. "One thing most of all."

"Now," Ignacio said. "We went over this. I ain't your priest."

The inmate nodded and looked at the ground.

"Okay then," Ignacio said. "As long as you know I got nothin for you."

"I want to be forgiven," the inmate said.

"We all want that," Ignacio said.

"You think she'd ever forgive me?" the inmate said.

"Don't know," Ignacio said. "I ain't even know who you're talkin about."

"You know it," the inmate said. "I ain't jus take that toe. I done more besides."

Ignacio nodded.

"Well," he said. "I suppose she might."

"Yeah?" the inmate said.

"Yeah," Ignacio said. "Now that it's done."

"How about you?" the inmate said. "If you was her pa?"

"No," Ignacio said. "I wouldn't."

"Not never?"

"Not never."

The inmate looked at the ground.

The rain beat down on the roof and there was an awful silence.

A small, black fly landed on Ignacio's neck and he swatted it.

"I want to be forgiven," the inmate said.

"You already said that," Ignacio said.

"I did cause it's true."

"Far as I can tell," Ignacio said, "forgiveness ain't ours to give."

"How'd you mean?" the inmate said.

"I mean," Ignacio said, "the only thing I've known a man to do is take his revenge."

"How about forgiveness?" the inmate said.

Ignacio spat.

"Ain't never seen it."

The inmate was silent. He looked down at the floor and coughed. Then he looked over at his fellow prisoner. Ignacio was pulling off his boots.

"Hey what you doin?" the inmate said.

Ignacio did not answer.

The inmate watched as he popped the heel off of his left boot.

"What's that?"

Inside of the shoe was a small, hollow cavity.

Ignacio emptied its contents into the palm of his hand.

"What you got there?"

Ignacio held out a self-contained pistol cartridge, a wick, and two pieces of flint.

"What's that for?"

Ignacio nodded toward the jailer who was asleep in his chair.

The inmate smiled.

Ignacio rose to his feet and walked to the cell door. He turned to the inmate.

"When he comes in, you let him hit you once or twice. Don't fight back."

"How's that?" the inmate said.

"Do what I say," Ignacio said. "And we'll be free men."

The inmate nodded.

Ignacio poured the contents of the cartridge into the cylinder of the lock. Then he put the wick in place and struck the flint. The flint sparked and lit the wick. With a single flash the lock busted open. Pieces of the locking mechanism went flying in every direction and the door swung on its hinges. The guard awoke and jumped to his feet. He rushed toward the cell and entered.

"You black bastard!" he yelled and he swung his fist at the inmate.

The inmate dodged the punch and struck him in the gut.

The guard heaved and swung again.

The inmate took a punch on the chin and he began swinging his arms wildly.

Meanwhile, Ignacio had left the cell to retrieve his club. It was hanging from a hook at the end of the hall. When he returned, the inmate was on top of the guard beating him savagely. Ignacio grabbed him by the collar and pushed him off. Then he stood over the guard and spat. The man was whimpering beneath him like a wounded animal. He looked helpless and pathetic. He raised his hands to shield his face but it was no use. Ignacio brought his club down like a mallet. It split the guard's head and fractured his skull. Ignacio raised his club. The guard convulsed. Ignacio brought it down again. The guard's skull broke in two. Ignacio raised his club. He brought it down. He raised his club. And brought it down. He pounded it over and over, up and down, until he had beaten through anything human and was just pounding, pounding on the muddy floor.

The inmate reached out and touched his shoulder.

Ignacio dropped his club.

He stood there gasping and heaving over the mud that once was a man. And when he was finally able to catch his breath, he turned and walked out into the darkness without saying another word.

❦

The red Arizona sun was just rising over the plains and the gray colt was making its long ascent up the side of the barren ridge. The climb was steep and Ignacio clung to the mane of the horse. He had ridden through the night from the whorehouse to the hills with nothing but the stars and a makeshift torch to light his way. He was sore and tired. His mouth was dry and his bones cracked and ached. He dug his heels into the ribs of the horse and urged it higher. It climbed and climbed and eventually came to a stop at a cleft in the rock. Ignacio dismounted and tied the horse to an old, rotted log. He patted it twice on the nose and entered the cave.

Inside, the flame from his torch was swallowed up by darkness. He could not see more than a few feet in front of him and all he could see was stone and black. He walked slowly, cautiously. The stink of sulfur filled his nose and he coughed and spat. Then a swarm of black bats with ugly red faces descended from the slate above. They screeched and beat their ugly wings. Ignacio ducked and swung his torch in terror. He shielded his face with one hand and tried to fend off the monsters with the other. They flapped against his arms and against his shirt. He felt one in his hair and another biting at the back of his neck. He screamed and his screams sent echoes reverberating down into the belly of the cavern. He dropped his torch. It fell into a puddle of stale water extinguishing what little light there had been. He rolled around in the dirt and the bats flew off shrieking. Then he laid there. Alone in the dark.

When he finally got up, he realized that there was nothing to do but continue on into the blackness. He rubbed his hands along the walls and felt his way forward. A few paces on he heard something. A familiar sound. The sound of water. *Drip drop. Drip drop drop.* His mouth salivated and he followed the noise until he came to a slip in the rock. He ran his palm over it. Water bubbled and dribbled out. It was cold and clear. He pursed his lips and pressed them to the stone. The liquid was like ice on his tongue and he patted his hands on the wall and rubbed them over his face. He panted and licked, panted and sipped. Then he leaned back and let out a long sigh.

From somewhere deep in the hollow of the cave came the faint glow of firelight. Ignacio sipped the water again and then set out to find it. As he approached an opening in the rock, he could see the fire dancing and smoking and licking the air. The wood cracked and hissed beneath the flames. Ash and embers whirled round and round like moths around a lantern. They sparked and jumped and glowed in the darkness. There was a man kneeling naked before the blaze. He was short and thin with gray scales on his face and neck. He knelt with his bare back to Ignacio. It was covered with lashes and bruises. His scrawny ass was red and swollen. The bottoms of his feet were charred as if he had been walking on fire. He held a knotted rope in one hand and a rosary in the other. He used the rope to flagellate himself and the rosary to pray. The orange glow of the flames accentuated the crimson of his blood and his body looked raw and emaciated.

"So ya've come at last," said Markel without turning.

Ignacio watched him from the shadows.

"Been waitin these six years. But he who waits waits on the lord. And the lord shan't grow weary. The lord renews all things."

Ignacio stared at the blood dripping from the monk's mutilated back. It ran like the water down the slip in the rock.

"Come," Markel said. "Help an old sinner to his feet."

Ignacio stepped out of the darkness into the light of the cave. He walked toward the flames and bent over to pick up the monk's hair shirt robe.

"No," Markel said. "Naked he came forth from his mother's womb and naked he'll return."

Ignacio dropped the robe and approached.

"Come," Markel said. "Give him yer hand."

Ignacio extended his hand.

Markel grabbed it. His grip was tight. He wrapped his pruney fingers around Ignacio's wrist and pulled himself to his feet. Then he stood there naked and bleeding in the firelight.

"Why do you look at him so?" Markel said. "Did our lord not see fit to be stripped and beaten? Did he not love to be mocked at and jeered? It's his blood that stains our hands. It's his blood that brings its curse upon us all. Shhh! Listen. It cries out. Ain't you hear it?"

The two stood in silence.

Then an echo came up from the belly of the cave like the shrieking of the bats.

"Who are you?" Ignacio said.

"He who'll be first must be last," Markel said. "The greatest, least. A slave to all."

Ignacio stared at the monk's clownish face. It was more hideous than he remembered. But behind it were those beautiful blue eyes. Alive and dead all at once. They were enough to make any man stop and listen.

"Come to give yer confession," Markel said. "And yet you come not with repentance but revenge in yer heart."

"I've come to ask you somethin," Ignacio said. "There's somethin I got to know."

"No," Markel said. "You ain't come here a yer own volition. It's the lord who bring you to this place. And yet yer the one who marks himself with the sign a the beast."

Ignacio looked at him intently.

"You carry it in yer belt. You sling it round yer shoulder. And you ain't never hesitate to bring it down on a man's head. Them scars bear witness to the power it lords over ya."

Ignacio stared into his clear, blue eyes.

They looked off aimlessly, gazing at nothing at all.

"It weighs on you," Markel said. "Like a millstone hung round yer neck."

"Who are you?" Ignacio said. "How do you know me?"

"He is who he is," Markel said. "He knows what god tells him. Nothin more. Lest he think himself wise and become a fool for the devil."

"What'd you know about them murders?" Ignacio said. "About them boys bein butchered in town?"

"There's but one murder," Markel said. "The murder a the lamb slaughtered before the foundation a the world. Every son a Cain forces his knife back through that lamb's heart."

Ignacio looked at him intently.

"One a them boys died near here. Found him at the bottom a the ridge."

"Aye," Markel said. "He knows. He sees."

"What do you see?"

"He sees the man who done it," Markel said. "He looks that man straight in his eyes."

"That so?" Ignacio said. "What's he look like?"

"Like the antichrist," Markel said. "Walkin round in human flesh."

"And you," Ignacio said. "What makes you burn

your feet black and flog yourself til you bleed?"

"Ah," Markel said. "Now he understands. You think this poor old monk had somethin to do with it."

"No," Ignacio said. "Not til I saw you kneelin there."

He studied Markel carefully, trying to discern what to believe.

"The monk knows the boy," Markel said. "That's true enough. A runaway who come to the hills lookin for repentance. The monk teaches him to fast, teaches him to pray. Teaches him to reject the world and all its trappins. But dry bones hurt no one. An old man can mortify his flesh. He can take the sufferin a the world into his body and marry himself to that cross. That ain't mean he hurt no boy."

"A man who scars himself will scar another," Ignacio said.

Markel laughed.

"You let someone else's words poison yer mouth," he said. "Is it really the wisdom a that wizard you've come to peddle?"

Ignacio looked at him with amazement.

"But the wisdom a the world is foolishness to god," Markel said. "You know it yerself. You've spent this most sacred of weeks offerin yer body as a sacrifice to the lord."

Ignacio could not explain why but for some reason he trusted the insane old man. It was as if his insanity revealed his innocence. And if he were innocent of the crimes, then he alone could lead Ignacio to the man who was guilty. It didn't make sense. But that was Ignacio's conviction.

"If you ain't killed them," Ignacio said. "Then who?"

"Another Cain," Markel said. "A man who give himself to the devil."

"What's he look like?"

"The lamp a the body's the eye," Markel said. "If yer eye's sound, yer body be filled with light. But if

81

yer eye's evil, yer body be cloaked in darkness. And if the light in yer eye's gone dark, how great'll that darkness be!"

"Show me," Ignacio said. "Teach me to see."

"To understand Cain," Markel said, "ya must become Cain. Or return to the dark you already was."

"How?"

"In the mind," Markel said. "And that offends god more than any sin a the flesh."

"I need to know," Ignacio said.

"The monk knows you do," Markel said. "Knows it's why you've come. But he warns ya. Be good and sure you can bear what's to be seen. Cause when you look long and hard into that dark, you might see nothin but yerself."

❦

Outside the church, the cold, black blood of Santino still stained the white desert earth. After the commotion had ended, his body had been dragged off and buried without ceremony. The wood was burnt, the chains washed and given to the blacksmith, the rosary thrown into the pit alongside their final owner. But a day later, the blood remained, a witness to the slaughter.

Maryellen stopped and crossed herself as she approached. She had known Santino in this life and was pained to think of how he had met his end. He had visited her at ma'am's on more than one occasion. He was too ashamed to have her see him naked and always made her turn away as he undressed. He would have her lay face down on the bed and when he was finished he would ask her to continue to lie there until he left. She felt sad for him but did not know why. Something in the way he touched. He seemed so helpless. Like a wounded animal. And she could tell that that helplessness had made him cruel.

When she entered the church, she found it empty. The fonts were dry and none of the candles were lit. She walked to the sacristy and peered in. There was no sign of the boy or of anyone else. She went to the back and ascended the stone stairs that led up to the bell tower. When she reached the top, she pushed open the wooden door and entered. It, too, was empty. She paused and looked out over the quiet Arizona desert. The first rays of sun spread like fingers across the land and the white moon still hung low in the morning sky. She looked west to the hills and wondered where Ignacio was. She hoped he was safe and feared he might be hurt. Or worse. Then she cursed her fears and cursed herself for allowing such fears to enter her head. She turned and descended the stairs.

When she reached the bottom, she noticed that the outer door was slightly ajar. She was sure that she had closed it when she entered. She walked around into the church and saw a man standing, staring up at the cross. He was a pale, stocky man with black hair and yellow eyes. She reached into her dress and gripped the handle of her gun.

"You," she said.

The man turned and fixed his eyes on her.

"My," he said. "You healed real nice."

"What do you want?"

"What all men want," he said. "Except I ain't afraid a what's goin to happen when I get it."

"Where's the boy?"

"You're pretty," he said. "I like the looks a you."

"Where is he?"

The man stepped toward her.

She pulled the pistol from her dress and pointed it at him.

He smiled.

"Now," he said. "We both know you ain't goin to use it."

"The boy," she said.

"Do you believe in fate?" the man said.

She looked at him over the barrel of the gun.

"Like things are written in the stars?"

Her hand was shaking.

"Never believed it myself," he said. "But here we are."

"Where is he?" she said.

"Funny how life works out," he said. "Some call it coincidence. I'm startin to think it might a been planned after all."

"I ain't goin to ask you again."

"Don't you worry about that boy," the man said. "He ain't none a your concern."

He took another step toward her.

"I'll do it," she said. "I'll shoot."

He smiled.

"Pretty when you're scared. Red cheeks. I like that."

There was a commotion outside. She could hear people running and shouting. There was panic and there were screams.

He took another step.

Bang! A shot rang out.

The bullet punched through the man's shoulder and he stumbled back.

Maryellen stood motionless, smoke rising from her gun.

The man let out a low grunt and he gritted his teeth.

"That's a mistake," he said. "You should a killed me."

The doors of the church flew open and a crowd of people came rushing in.

"Quick!" one said. "Bar the doors!"

"Injuns!" another said. "Apache!"

❧❧❧

Brother Markel led Ignacio through a series of passages deep into the belly of the rock. There were crude etchings on the walls that depicted monstrous animals—horned, hoofed, with black eyes, feathered wings, and jagged, bloodstained teeth. There were words scratched into the stone in an odd, primitive script that Ignacio could not read. There were images of the sun and moon and one of a bare breasted woman with serene eyes and blood flowing from her hands and feet. There was a child wrapped around her hips and he hid his face in her naked thigh.

As they walked, Markel chanted the *Attende Domine*. His voice echoed down into the heart of the cave and it reverberated back. He walked by memory, stepping over stones, ducking when the ceiling was low, turning sideways to squeeze through the narrow bends in the path. He led Ignacio to another opening in the rock. It was lit only by candlelight.

"Come," Markel said. "See the place prepared fer a poor sinner by the lord."

It was a small crypt cut into the stone by the Jesuit missions some two hundred years before. An ornate gold cross hung over a large, flat rock, apparently meant to be used as an altar. The candles were old and burnt low. Melted wax hardened into dry driblets on the granite. The walls were lined with the bones of dead priests. Ribs, limbs, skulls with broken teeth and eyeless sockets, fingers, toes, jawbones, joints—all fixed to the stone without place or purpose. They were arranged in no particular order. As meaningless as the men they had once held erect.

Laid out on the altar was an old, worn book of prayers and next to it were a gold chalice and a monstrance which held a piece of dry bread.

Ignacio genuflected and blessed himself.

"The lord's always here," Markel said. "Always watchin."

"This is where you pray?"

"The monk offers mass," Markel said. "Each day at dawn. And he waits on the whisper a the lord."

"What would you have me do?"

"Eat this," Markel said.

He handed him the dry roots of a plant.

"What is it?"

"Eat it," Markel said. "And kneel before the sacrament."

Ignacio took the plant and put it in his mouth. He knelt down and began to chew.

The monk turned and walked toward the passage from which they had come.

"Where are you going?" Ignacio said.

"Ask the lord fer what you seek," the monk said. "He'll show you the way."

"Stay," Ignacio said.

"No," Markel said. "You must do it alone."

He turned and walked out.

Ignacio closed his eyes and began to pray. When he opened them again, the crypt seemed darker. He looked up at the cross. It was smaller than he remembered. And the walls seemed closer too. He began breathing heavily and worried that the room was running out of air. He felt sweat bead on his brow and he was certain that one of the skulls was staring at him through its eyeless sockets. He wanted to smash it with his club. Then he heard Markel enter and walk up behind him. He was relieved to not be alone and wanted to turn to greet the old monk. But he could not turn. His arms and legs refused to work. His neck was stiff, his head fixed in place. He was completely paralyzed. He thought to scream out but could not open his mouth. The man behind him walked closer and he realized it was not Markel. It was some dark figure.

The crypt grew darker still and the man moved closer. Ignacio was filled with terror. He felt the man's hands press in on his ribs. He could not breathe and the man squeezed and he thought that he would be crushed. He tried to cry out but the man forced a gag into his throat and he choked and gasped for air. He spit the gag from his mouth and began screaming wildly.

"In Christ's name!" he yelled. "In the name of Jesus and his holy blood."

For a moment, all went silent. Ignacio tried to steady his breathing and calm his thoughts. But suddenly he felt himself being pulled backwards as if falling from a ledge. He fell down, down into the darkness and he knew that the man was waiting at the bottom and that there was no escape.

"In the name of Christ Jesus!" he said. "By our savior's blood!"

Again all was silent and he was alone in the crypt. He tried to make sense of what was happening but no sense would come. He closed his eyes and it was night. He opened them and it was day. At one moment he was kneeling. Then standing. Then sitting. Then suspended in the air above the room. He was in the crypt, then in the desert, then behind bars in a Texas prison. He could not focus on any one thing and felt rather that everything was swept up in a chaotic flux. All things, he thought, are spiraling down, down toward their oblivion. All is for naught. The nothing is coming. It's coming for me. He began to weep bitterly and pulled on his face. He tugged at his hair and ground his teeth and terror gripped his heart. He closed his eyes and when he opened them again he was standing in the middle of the crypt and all was silent. He looked from wall to wall at the dead men's bones. How dry they were. Then he heard a voice, horrible and familiar.

"Can these bones come back to life?" said the man.

But Ignacio could not answer. His thoughts were drowned out by the rattle of bones as joint fit to joint and the skeletons pieced themselves together. They stood before him lipless and awful, grinning because they could not help but grin. He trembled as tendons and ligaments grew out of the bones, connecting them one to the other. Then they grew skin. Then hair and garments to cover their naked flesh. They were completely still. A vast and terrible army. And the man chuckled and his chuckle spread from ear to ear. It rang in Ignacio's brain and he closed his eyes and tried hard to wake himself from the vision. Instead he heard a noise like the charging of bulls and felt himself being pulled in every direction. The horde of hooded men came running. They seized him with their wretched hands and tugged on his arms and legs. They clawed at his flesh and yanked him this way and that.

God, he thought, has forsaken me. I am alone. And this is my death.

He felt their fingers pulling and tearing and picking at his skin. Their nails cut him and they bit and chewed and gnawed on his bones. He could not see or hear or think and all he could do was cry and suck at the air. Then he was met by a pair of cold, yellow eyes and he fixed his gaze upon them. They were dark and full of terror—the kind of eyes that could look upon all that god had made and say that it was a mistake. The kind of eyes that could prove it. Ignacio looked into those eyes and he saw that they were his eyes and that he was looking at his own reflection.

Then he awoke and he was no longer in the cave.

The air outside was cool and the sky clear. It was night and the dome above shined like water and the stars stood forth in all their glory. Ignacio sat up and scratched his head. He was alone at the bottom of the ridge and the gray colt was a few yards off grazing on a patch of dry grass. He looked at the hills behind him. The dim glow of firelight flickered from a cleft in the rock. He looked east toward the town. There was a pillar of smoke on the horizon but he could not see where it was coming from.

"So," Ignacio said. "It was you all along."

Then he stood, walked to his horse, mounted it, and rode away.

D eep in the hollow of the rock, a mass was being offered. It was just after dawn on Holy Thursday and Brother Markel had been on his knees in prayer since the night before. He was alone, chanting and singing and speaking in tongues. His voice echoed off the walls and off the ceiling and if anyone had been there he would have sworn that Markel was not alone and that the voices that echoed back were not his. Throughout the service, his sightless eyes looked down at his hands, old and withered. Hands that had done much and had more to do. Above the stone altar hung a gold crucifix. Draped over the crucifix was a dark purple cloth. It hid the cross and the god nailed to it. And the monstrance was covered. And the candles had not been lit. And the book of prayers was closed shut.

Markel rose and walked to the altar. He bowed down and kissed it. Then he turned and proclaimed the day's gospel. He spoke clearly, boldly. He knew the reading by heart and recited it without error. He told the story of how, on the eve of his death, Jesus had washed his disciples' feet, of how Peter had refused at first but ultimately relented, of how Jesus insisted that his followers go and do the same. Then he sang the *Alleluia*. Then he began to preach.

"Brothers and sisters," he said to the stone. "This day, Christians the world over gather together to kneel and pray and offer the eucharist in remembrance a the lord. This is how you remember me, he says. Til I come again. And so we do remember. We live on memories. We feed on memories. Our thirst quenched with memories. Memories and forgettin. Memories and pain. Memories and the dark.

"Today be Holy Thursdy. The Thursdy a mysteries.

And it ain't no accident that on this day the church instruct us to veil the cross. It ain't no accident that she tell us to conceal it, to keep it hidden, to cover it with our shame. It might seem like a strange practice. But it ain't. The church be wiser than we know. She be more honest. More true.

"Scripture tell us that the fool say in his heart there ain't no god. But today, brothers and sisters, god make that fool wise. Today, god hide himself, conceal himself, leave us with nothin but memories. Memories and the dark.

"You hear it said from time to time. One man say to the other how faith make for a good crutch. Sometimes it's easy to believe. Sometimes you ain't like what's true. But the truth that god give us this day is a truth that no man want to believe. The truth he give ain't no truth at all. Today god ask us to believe in nothin. Today he ask us to believe in the dark. Sacrifice, says the lord. Sacrifice everythin that comfort. Everythin holy, healin, sacred, true. Sacrifice yer belief. Sacrifice yer god, even. Yer idea a god. And out a cruelty to yerself, worship stone, fate, stupidity, the nothin. Sacrifice yer god to the nothin. Then sacrifice yerself.

"He ask this, he demand it, not because he ain't here, not because he ain't listenin, not because he ain't true. He ask it because we ain't here. We ain't listenin. We ain't true. At least, we ain't want to be. The nothin, says the lord. That is you. And if you ain't see it, you ain't know yer own heart. The nothin is you and it's bigger than you. It's the powers a this world. It's the powers that drag you down into the dark. It's the cosmic struggle. The pain, the emptiness, the sufferin, the death. It's happenin all around us. Whether you see that or not. It's the darkness and the lord alone is the light.

"Evil, brothers and sisters, is a great mystery. The

depths a horror run deeper than anythin human. The brutality a this world is unthinkable to the mind a man. But not his heart. A heart that can give itself over to the diabolic. A heart that can be corrupted by the spirit a the antichrist. A heart made so free it can bind itself to its own destruction. That heart lies at the center a man. That heart drives him, guides him, corrupts him.

"Make no mistake. The antichrist is real. As real as anyone in this room. He's spirit. A power a this world. And he walks the earth in human flesh. He plants himself in the heart a man. He makes a hole, a black spot, a stain. He makes a void without end. From there he inflicts his menace. From there he sets loose his murderous ways. He fixes himself and spreads like a plague, destroyin everythin in his path. He strips us a our humanity. He steals our dignity. He mars the image a the creator written in our hearts. He's the reason god chooses the nothin. The reason god enters the void. The reason he becomes like us and bears our sins. This antichrist lives in every man. And god won't have it. So he takes it on himself.

"Sacrifice, says the lord. Sacrifice everythin. Even yer hope. Even yer belief. Even yer god. And once you've abandoned all, once you've given up yer desire, yer longin, yer happiness, yer salvation, once you've forsaken and been forsaken—then it's time to believe. Then it's time for faith. Not an easy faith. Not a crutch. A faith that rises out a nothin. A faith deeper than the abyss. A faith born from the death a god himself.

"Today, brothers and sisters, we kneel and we pray and we remember. We remember the god we ain't see, the god we ain't touch, the god who veil himself behind purple and behind our shame. That god don't make nothin easy. Especially faith. That god leave us with the ghost a god, the shadow a god, the absence a god. And nothin more. He leave us the nothin and he ask us to believe. He leave us the darkness and he ask us to trust. He ask us to know that he hears our prayers, our sighs, the blood that cries out. He ask us to trust in his love even as we bury the knife. That ain't easy. That ain't no crutch. And in these dark days a lent, we're reminded all the more a just how forsaken we really is. We're reminded that we forsook ourselves."

The old monk paused to catch his breath.

"And yet this loneliness," he continued. "This sufferin, this dark—this, my dear brothers and sisters, is the faith we're called to live. This is the joy a the saints and the strength a the martyrs. This is the glory and the triumph a the lord. The god who hides himself reveals himself in the dark. He speaks in silence. He's present in absence. His blood cries out. This is our great hope. This is the mystery a faith. And we must bear it. We must cling to it. For if we open ourselves, if we look hard and deep into that abyss, we may just find that out a nothin comes somethin, out a void comes fullness, out a darkness comes the light and the life a the world. Our abyss ain't no dark abyss. It is our salvation.

"God bless ye and keep ye durin these tryin days. Amen."

When he had finished, he walked to the altar and performed the rest of the service in silence—blessing, consecrating, genuflecting, raising host and chalice high in the air, breaking the host into the chalice and preparing to consume. Then after chanting the "Agnus Dei" and placing the host on his tongue, he fell to the ground convulsing and went unconscious.

Blood and hoofprints in the sand and black smoke billowing on the horizon. The screams of the dying and the silence of the dead. Vultures circling in the air above, squawking and beating their wings. The low, dull hum of flies that leap from corpse to corpse and nest in burnt and rotting flesh. Blood in pools — spattered on trees, caked on walls and doors. Black blood dried and congealed in the streets like pudding. Smoldering embers. Houses razed to the ground. Broken arrows and shotgun shells in the dust. Screaming colts with shattered bones and dead indians with bullet holes in their chests. Whores who have been dragged out and raped under the hot sun. Stones used as weapons, makeshift clubs. A child crying in a doorway. A woman stripped naked, her scalp peeled back. Men without heads. Others without limbs. Some castrated and left to bleed out in the sand. The stench of death and of rotting flesh. The wind blowing across the plain and the smell of lilac in the bush.

Ignacio urged his horse on through the carnage. He had witnessed scenes like this before and knew that the chances of survival were bleak. Still, he had hope and he clung to it.

When he got to ma'am's place, he could see that the windows had been smashed and the door torn off its hinges. There was a dead prostitute out front who had been bound hand and foot and made to crawl through the dirt while her attackers shot arrows at her. There was the tattered body of an apache full of bullet holes and a young girl lying naked with a knife in her gut. There were broken bottles on the steps and blood and piss on the porch. There was a coyote sniffing around out back and flies buzzing in the air above and the place reeked of sex and booze and death.

Ignacio tied his horse to a tree and mounted the stairs. He held the carbine at his waist with his finger on the trigger. He entered through the doorless frame, stepping over the cold, slouched body of a girl sprawled out in the foyer. Inside, the house was damp and musty. There were dead men and dead whores everywhere. Some went quick with an arrow through the heart. Others were beaten and tortured with their scalps pulled back to the skull. One leaned forward on the piano with a hatchet in his neck and his face pressed down on the keys. Ignacio seemed to hear a long, dead note ringing out. He walked over and pushed him off with his boot. The room was silent. Then a mangy black cat with oily black fur scurried past. Then another approached and rubbed itself against Ignacio's leg. He looked down at it and it purred. He kicked it and it hissed and he walked to the bar. There he found the cold, lifeless body of ma'am lying in a pool of dry blood. Her face was mutilated. The top half of her skull had been blown off by a shot from a Derringer. The gun was in her hand and her finger was still on the trigger. Ignacio spat and thought of the carnage she had spared herself by not being afraid to use it. And the carnage she inflicted.

In one of the rooms, he found the doctor. The man had hidden himself under a bed and died when his attacker thrust his spear down through the mattress. He was pinned to the floor with his face looking up as if he had watched the man's feet and had known the outcome even before it forced itself down upon him. His clothes were in a pile in the corner of the room. His whore was lying dead, sprawled out by the window. She was pregnant and her child had been cut from her abdomen. It lay strange and alien on the ground by her womb.

As Ignacio mounted the stairs to the upper bedrooms, his heart began to race. He paused at the top and listened. There was a low, muffled noise like breathing coming from the room at the end of the hall. He walked slowly, deliberately. When he got to the door, he pushed it open with the nose of his rifle. There lying bloody and wounded on Maryellen's bed was an apache, face streaked with war paint and blood. He looked at Ignacio with pain in his eyes. There was a bullet hole in his gut and blood on the sheets.

"The girl," Ignacio said. "Where is she?"

The man winced.

"Where?" Ignacio said.

The man coughed and blood poured from his mouth.

Ignacio pulled the door shut and walked away.

He exited the house, slung his rifle over one shoulder, his club over the other, mounted his horse, and rode on into town.

❦

It was a summer night in 1850 when Ignacio and the inmate with whom he'd escaped from a Texas prison finally found the other bounty hunter's lodgings. The rain had slowed to a drizzle and the two prisoners had walked for miles through the Texas wetlands. The storm had caused flooding and the roads and byways were mud and the prisoners were wet and their boots were soaked through. They came to a small inn on the outskirts of town and saw the other bounty hunter's horse tied to a post under an overhang where it could take shelter from the storm. The horse neighed and kicked and the two approached and ducked down under a nearby tree.

"You wait here," Ignacio said to the inmate. "I'll be back soon."

"What'm I doin here?"

"Waitin," Ignacio said. "And this time you listen."

"I listened befo."

"You ain't. I told you not to fight back."

"Yeah, well, it's easy to say," the inmate said. "But that ain't make it easy to do."

"I suppose not," Ignacio said. "And I suppose I

don't give a damn. Do what I say if you want a live. And if you don't, well then you're on your own."

"Been on my own my whole life," the inmate said. "Why's it goin to change now?"

"You do what you want," Ignacio said. "Stay or go. Just don't get in the way."

"I'll stay," the inmate said. "I'll wait for you."

"Well, there we go," Ignacio said. "I knew I liked you."

The inmate smiled.

Ignacio spat.

"What you goin to tell him?" the inmate said.

"I ain't goin to tell him much."

"Goin to let that club do the talkin?"

"Alright," Ignacio said. "That's enough out a you. I'm goin in there."

"Wait," the inmate said.

"What is it?" Ignacio said.

"I like you too," the inmate said. "Wanted you to know it."

"I know it," Ignacio said.

He spat and walked away.

When he got to the door, he knocked three times on the outer grating.

"What you want?" came a voice from the other side.

"Need a room."

"We're full."

"It's wet. I'll pay double."

"We're full."

"How much?"

"Go on," the voice said. "Get."

"Okay," Ignacio said. "If that's how it is."

He walked about ten paces from the door, turned, lowered his shoulder, and charged at it as fast as he could. Bang! He broke clear through and stumbled in. He collected himself, grabbed the doorman by the

97

throat, wrestled a pistol out of his hand, and pressed it against his temple.

"Don't you move," he said. "Or I'll spray your brains all over this fuckin room."

"Fuck you," the doorman said.

So Ignacio raised his hand and brought the butt of the gun down on his head.

It split the doorman's head open and he cried out in pain.

"Shut up," Ignacio said. "Or you'll get another."

The doorman stopped struggling and went quiet.

"John!" Ignacio said. "I know you're here."

All was still.

"John," Ignacio said. "I came to make my fuss."

The other bounty hunter emerged from one of the bedrooms with a shotgun in his hands.

"Well," he said. "What's this?"

"You know what it is," Ignacio said. "You know why I come."

"I do," the bounty hunter said. "But I ain't know what you're expectin to get."

"I want two things," Ignacio said.

"Yeah?" the bounty hunter said. "What's that?"

"First, I want my freedom. I want to be left alone."

"Freedom?" the bounty hunter laughed. "Freedom ain't nothin but a story we tell."

"It's my story," Ignacio said. "And I plan on doin the tellin."

The bounty hunter spat.

"And next, I want to make you a rich man."

"Yeah?" the bounty hunter said. "How you fixin to do that?"

"I got money," Ignacio said. "Lots a money."

"And?" the bounty hunter said.

"And I'm goin to give it all to you."

"What for?" the bounty hunter said.

"To be left alone. For my freedom."

"Now," the bounty hunter said. "You're askin for things I can't rightly give."

"I'm askin for the names a them indian fellas who want me dead. You tell me their names and I'll do the rest."

"Now," the bounty hunter said. "You know I can't do that."

"You can," Ignacio said.

"Well," the bounty hunter said. "You know I ain't about to."

"John," Ignacio said. "You know me. You know I'm a man a my word."

"I know it," the bounty hunter said.

"Then listen when I tell you I got money. Four thousand buried and hid well."

"I'm listenin," the bounty hunter said.

"And I got a negro outside. There's a three hundred dollar tag on his head. It's all yours if you help me do this."

"Forty-three hundred?" the bounty hunter said.

"Forty-three hundred," Ignacio said. "Four thousand tonight. Three hundred when you bring that boy home in chains."

"And why would I do that?" the bounty hunter said.

"You told me once that you was fixin to quit this business. You told me you wanted to head out west. Settle down. Maybe play the part a lawman for a while. Ain't you want to do somethin more honest?"

"Now," the bounty hunter said. "We both know it ain't no more honest."

"More respectable then."

The bounty hunter nodded.

"How do I know I can trust you?"

"You can trust me," Ignacio said.

"No," the bounty hunter said. "I want proof."

"I ain't got none to give."

"Sure you do," the bounty hunter said. "Tell me

a story."

"What kind a story?"

"I want a good story," the bounty hunter said. "I want to hear about how you got that scar."

"What's that got to do with it?"

"If you can't trust a man with small things," the bounty hunter said, "you can't trust him with big ones."

"And if that's a big one?" Ignacio said.

"Even better," the bounty hunter said.

"You want a story?" Ignacio said.

The bounty hunter nodded.

"And if I tell it and if you believe it, you'll take the money and let me go?"

The bounty hunter nodded once more.

"Okay, then," Ignacio said. "Here goes."

The two lowered their guns and sat down at a table. The bounty hunter handed the doorman a bag of coins to make up for the trouble and he had him bring out a bottle of whiskey. They drank and talked for over an hour. And when they emerged from the inn, they walked to the tree, pointed their guns at the inmate, bound him hand and foot, and the three rode off into the darkness together.

❦

When he got to the center of town, Ignacio found more of the same. Dead bodies piled in the streets and blood on every corner. Black smoke still rose like incense to the sky and he thought of the burnt offerings of old and of the sacrifices meant to cover our sins. He followed the smoke until he came to the old Spanish church. Then he got down from his horse and fell to his knees and he wept bitterly. The church lay in ashes on the ground. Smoldering stones and red hot embers were all that was left.

"Hey," the lawman called from a short distance

away. "I'm dyin."

Ignacio turned and saw him leaned up against a nearby rock. He had an arrow in his chest and another in his side and he wheezed and sucked at the air.

Ignacio wiped his face. Then he rose to his feet and walked over.

"Got any water?" the lawman said.

Ignacio walked back to his horse and grabbed a canteen. He returned and handed it to the dying man.

The lawman drank it greedily and he poured it over his sunburnt face. Then he coughed and spit blood.

"Thank you," he said. "I needed it."

Ignacio nodded.

"You're alive," the lawman said. "Glad to see it."

"What happened?" Ignacio said.

"Injuns," the lawman said.

"Apache?" Ignacio said.

"Apache," the lawman said.

"What happened?"

"The townsfolk," the lawman said. "Ain't none a them believe you killed them boys. Swore it was the injuns. So they formed a posse and went lookin for trouble."

"They found it," Ignacio said.

"They brought it here," the lawman said.

"The girl," Ignacio said. "Maryellen."

"Your girl," the lawman said. "I seen her."

"Where?" Ignacio said.

"Here," the lawman said. "When I got to the church."

"Was she..." Ignacio paused and looked off at the horizon.

"No," the lawman said. "I don't think so."

"What happened to her?"

"When I got here," the lawman said, "the church

was on fire. There was injuns runnin round hollerin in their strange tongue. And there was townsfolk runnin and hidin and tryin to fight em off. The church was burnin and the roof was cavin in. I was firin my rifle tryin to kill as many as I could but in all that terror I lost track and started shootin anythin that moved. I ain't even know who it was."

"Then what?"

"Then the roof caved in," the lawman said. "There was a loud crack like a canon bein fired and a big cloud a smoke filled the air. Everyone stopped and watched it burn, all a us—even the injuns. We all just stood and watched it burn."

"And then?"

"Then I saw her," the lawman said. "She was with him. The man who beat her up so bad. He had her slung over his shoulder and she was just danglin there. Not dead but not alive neither. Not movin. Like a stuffed doll or somethin. He carried her off and the fightin continued. I killed a lot a them. And then they killed me."

"Where'd he take her?"

"To the hills," the lawman said. "To the desert. I don't know. But he carried her right out a that church. Come walkin straight through the flames. Like a devil walkin out a hell. Not a scratch on him. And the apache ain't get him neither. No one did. I'm the only one who saw it happen."

"You sure?" Ignacio said.

"I'm sure," the lawman said.

Ignacio nodded and spat.

"That man," the lawman said. "He's the one who killed them boys."

"How do you know it?"

"I know it," the lawman said. "Somethin about his face. Somethin about how he looked when he come walkin out a them flames. That man is the most unhappy man on earth. He's damned. He's in hell."

Ignacio nodded.

The two sat in silence and the wind blew through the brush.

"Father," the lawman said.

"Yeah?" Ignacio said.

"I got regrets," the lawman said.

"A man with no regrets," Ignacio said, "is a man who don't know himself."

"You think he'll forgive me?" the lawman said.

"I suppose he might."

"Yeah?" the lawman said.

"Yeah," Ignacio said. "Now that it's done."

"What about you?" the lawman said. "Do you forgive me?"

"Yeah," Ignacio said. "But only cause you're dyin."

The lawman coughed and blood poured from his mouth.

"Where's the sheriff?" Ignacio said. "Where's John?"

"He didn't make it," the lawman said.

Ignacio crossed himself.

"No one made it," the lawman said.

"You sure?" Ignacio said.

"I'm sure," the lawman said. "It's just you and the two a them. That's all that's left."

"Did you see the boy?" Ignacio said.

"What boy?" the lawman said.

"My altar boy," Ignacio said. "Bernardo."

"No," the lawman said. "I ain't seen him."

"Okay," Ignacio said. "I best be goin."

"Wait," the lawman said.

"What?" Ignacio said.

"Stay with me," the lawman said. "Just for a minute."

"Okay," Ignacio said.

"Okay," the lawman said.

Ignacio bent down and closed the man's eyes with

his fingers. He rubbed his palm over his brow and tried to comfort him as best he could. The lawman took a few deep breaths. Then his breathing slowed and slowed and his skin turned pale and he curled up and died. Ignacio blessed himself and made the sign of the cross over the dead man's body. He stood and walked back toward the church. Then he noticed something. A pair of boot prints pressed deep into the red desert earth. They were made by a man who had been carrying a heavy load. A man with a girl slung over his shoulder. They walked on into the wild in the direction of the silver mines. Ignacio checked his rifle and his pistol and he mounted his horse. Then he set out riding and followed the prints into the heat of the noonday sun.

❦

"Hey, boy," said the man. "Come here."

The altar boy looked at him hesitantly.

"I ain't askin," the man said. "Come here."

The boy rose to his feet and walked over.

"You see that down there?" the man said. "That little glimmer a light just beyond the bottom a the ridge?"

The boy looked out at the quiet Arizona desert. The sun above was high and hot. It bathed everything in incandescent light. There was smoke still rising from the ashes of the fallen church and there were birds of prey still circling over the town.

"What do you suppose that is?" the man said.

The boy continued to look.

"Asked you a question," the man said. "Best be answerin."

"I don't know," the boy said.

"I'll tell you what it is," the man said. "That there's the sun reflectin off the barrel of a rifle."

The boy looked hard but he could not see what

the man was talking about.

"Who do you think's carryin that rifle?" the man said.

"I don't know," the boy said.

"I'll tell you who," the man said. "Your priest."

"What if he is?" the boy said.

"If he is," the man said, "then we're gonna have a few surprises for him when he gets here."

"What if he's got a surprise for you?" the boy said.

The man looked at him intently.

"And what might that be?"

"What if he kills you dead? What if he uses that rifle to blow you to hell?"

The man smiled.

"That's good," he said. "I like that."

He patted the boy on the back.

The boy cringed and pulled away.

"Come," said the man. "Let's go see our mama. See how she's doin in there."

"No," the boy said.

"Come," said the man. "I ain't askin."

"No," the boy said.

"Boy," the man said. "You know what I done to her?"

The boy looked down at the dirt.

"You know what I'm fixin to do?"

The boy did not respond.

"You know that you're next?"

The boy began to shake.

"Unless," the man said, "you do everythin I say. Then maybe I'll spare you. But that's only cause I got a kind spot in my heart."

The boy continued to stare at the dirt.

"How about this," the man said. "From now on you call me pa?"

He put his hand on the boy's head and mussed his hair.

The boy did not move.

"Go on," the man said. "Call me pa."

The boy remained still.

"Call me pa."

"No," the boy said.

"I ain't askin," the man said.

"No," the boy said. "You ain't my pa."

The man smiled.

"I like you," he said. "You remind me a myself as a boy. And someday you'll be just like me."

The boy spat.

"Okay then," the man said. "But I ain't goin to forget it."

"Go away," the boy said.

"Come now," the man said. "That ain't nice."

"Go away," the boy said. "I hate you."

"Okay," the man said. "That's good. I get that too."

He turned and walked back toward the mineshaft.

"Hey, boy," he said. "Before I forget. You know what tomorrow is?"

The boy did not answer.

"I said you know what tomorrow is?"

"I know it," the boy said.

"What then?" the man said.

"Good Friday," the boy said.

"Speak up," the man said. "I ain't quite hear you."

"Good Friday," the boy said.

"Good Friday," the man said. "Goin to be a good Friday. Yes, sir, a real good Friday indeed."

❧❦❧

When nightfall came, Ignacio made his camp out under the stars. He knew that he was being watched from the mines above and he knew that there was nothing he could do about it. He did not attempt to hide. He did not look for a hole or a crevice in the rock. Instead, he built a fire large enough to ward off any hungry animals and resigned himself to the fact that god had seen fit to place him at a severe disadvantage. He was tired, wounded, hungry, old. In the morning, he would have to fight uphill against an enemy who was younger, stronger, and more cunning than he. There was no reason to believe he could win. And in many ways, he had already lost.

That night he fed on berries and on the roots of wild plants. He took off his boots and washed his feet in a small brook. He drank the last bit of water from his canteen and thought of the lawman with whom he'd shared this final drink. He closed his eyes and imagined the faces of the people in town. He saw them laughing, talking, joking with one another. He thought of how many he had served, how many he had befriended, how many he had loved. All undone by the blackness of death. He thought of her face, too, and he wished more than anything that he had kissed her. He wished that he could go back and kiss her now. What he would not give to kiss her now.

Then he knelt down and began to pray.

"Lord," he said, "tonight I pray in the common tongue and I am a common man. Tomorrow I intend to do the one thing I swore I'd never do again. I intend to swing my club and to spill another man's blood. I ask you not for your blessin. I've come to know you well enough to know that you'd never give it. I ask not even for your forgiveness. Who can forgive a man who breaks his word? I ask only that you understand. Know that I ain't want to do it. Know that I have to. And if you see fit, let me bear the consequence. Let me take the weight a this sin upon myself. Let me be crushed by it. And not this sin alone but the sin a the man I kill. The sin a each and every man I kill when I kill him. For it's all one sin, lord. And it's all one man. It's the sin a Cain. It's the sin a Adam. It's the murder a the lamb. One sin and one death. I ain't goin to deny it. I ain't goin to pretend like I don't know the truth. I only ask that you let it be poured out on me. Let your wrath be poured out on me. And if it's your will—help me bear it."

When he was done, he crossed himself and looked up at the sky. He thought of how god had created the heavens and the earth, the sun and moon and stars, the vastness of it all. How he had pulled everything out of nothing. How he had willed into existence that which never would have existed but for his willing. How he had set the whole drama of the universe in motion. Then he looked down at his hands and wondered why. Why had god done it? Why had he willed it to be? And why had he allowed a blackness, a trace of that nothing from which the world was created, to enter back in? Man was the center of the cosmos. Made in the image and likeness of his god. And at the center of man, right in the middle of his heart, was a hole—bottomless and empty. And there was nothing to fill that hole but whiskey and the void.

Ignacio laid his head on the dry grass next to the fire and fell asleep. He slept straight through the night and did not wake until the morning. And when he did, he knew his hour had come.

GOOD FRIDAY 🌺

Ignacio was awakened by a flash of lightning and a damp gust bringing rain. For the whole of Lent, the town had sat dry and barren under the curse of the red sun, that monstrous god of old. But now black clouds gathered and water dribbled from the sky like milk from a mother's breast. It cooled the land, stirred dull roots, extinguished hot embers, washed dry blood from hands and houses. He sat up and looked at the sky. There was no sun to be found. Only clouds and a cool mist rolling in from the slopes above. He put his fingers through his hair and thought of the last time he had felt rain on his scalp and of how strange it was that the rain should come on a day like this. On Good Friday. The day of his reckoning.

"Father," the altar boy called from a distance.

Ignacio turned and faced him.

"Don't do it," the boy said. "Don't come after us."

"Bernardo," Ignacio said.

He rose to his feet.

"No," the boy said. "You don't know this man. Don't come."

"A man's a man," Ignacio said. "I've known my share."

"No," the boy said. "This man ain't no man at all."

He turned and ran off into the desert grass.

"Wait," Ignacio called after him but the boy did not stop. He continued up the hill and out of sight. Ignacio knew he had been sent by the man, knew the man was watching from somewhere in the hills. He was trying to lure Ignacio into a trap. But Ignacio did not know how. He did not know what to look for, what to expect. Did the man want him to follow the boy up the side of the ridge? Did he think he would run straight into his clutches? Or did he know that Ignacio would hesitate? Did he want the priest to wait and think and consider? Did he want him to do exactly what he was doing right now?

"Lord," Ignacio said, "I don't know what's right and what's wrong. I don't know that you do neither. But guide me all the same. And whatever you want to have happen—let it be."

He bent down and picked up his rifle. It was wet with rain and he blew on the barrel and wiped it with his sleeve. Then he looked up the hillside toward the mines and wondered what the man was planning to do. He thought of Alexei and of the hangman and Santino. He thought of how they died and of how dead their bodies looked and of the hell they must have endured before they were buried in the cold, dry ground. A shiver went up his spine and he coughed and spat. Then he smiled. The boy's alive, he thought. And that's a reason to be grateful.

❧❦❧

The man stood out on a ledge and watched the boy make his way back up the hillside. He looked at him over the barrel of his gun, finger on the trigger. A stray bird flew past and it squawked in the damp desert air. The man lifted his gun and fired. His bullet split the bird in two and it fell dead on the spot. He lowered his gun, blew the smoke from the barrel, and spat. Then he looked back down the hill and saw Ignacio standing there, considering what to do. He smiled and reloaded and aimed his gun at the old priest. Then he pretended to fire.

"Bang," he said. "Bang."

He smiled again and dropped the gun to his side.

"The time is comin," he said. "Oh, it's comin."

He turned and walked into the mine cut out of the rock behind him. It was dark and damp and it smelled of sulfur and oil. There was a small fire burning in the corner and there were rusty metal tools piled up next to it. Picks, shovels, lanterns, an old hammer and a bucket of nails, an axe with a dull, orange blade, a stack of wooden railroad ties that were eight feet long and two feet wide. There were chisels and mallets and railroad spikes and next to the tools was a dark, black hole blown deep into the jagged rock. It was an abandoned mineshaft that led straight down into the bowels of the earth. The man walked to the edge of the shaft and peered in. He kicked a stone with his foot and it descended down into the darkness below. But he did not hear it hit. There was no bottom in sight.

Then he walked to the girl and bent down. He touched her cheek.

"Mornin, mama," he said.

Maryellen looked up in terror. Her hands were bound and her feet were bound and she was stripped naked. There was a gag stuffed in her mouth and she was on her knees, crouched down with her face in the dirt. She had bruises and lashes all over her pale white body and she had been beaten and tortured and starved half to death.

"I said mornin, mama. Where's your manners?"

She let out a muffled cry and covered her face with her hands.

"Remember when we first met?" the man said. "Not even one week ago."

She looked at him nervously.

"Remember what I told you that night? What I was sayin before I started hittin you?"

He took her hair in his hand, lifted it to his nose, and breathed in. It smelled sweet like perfume powder and lavender and he smiled and brushed it behind her ear.

"What was I sayin?" he said. "What'd I keep sayin?"

She looked up and trembled.

"Go on," he said. "I ain't goin to hurt you. Not yet."

He took the gag from her mouth and grinned an ugly grin.

"You said," she said.

"Go on," he said.

"You said," she said. "That I was pretty."

"You is pretty, mama," he said. "Real pretty."

"You said," she said. "I was too pretty."

"Too pretty for what?"

She cringed.

"Go on," he said. "I want to see if you remember."

"I remember," she said.

"Go on," he said. "Too pretty for what?"

She looked away.

"Too pretty for what?"

"Too pretty to fuck."

"That's right," he said. "I said we needed to ugly you up."

She began to whimper.

"What's a matter, mama?" he said. "Ain't you know how to take a compliment?"

She was shaking and heaving and tears poured like blood from her face.

"Don't worry," he said. "You're almost there. Just a while longer. But the time's comin. It's comin soon."

She lowered her head.

"And besides," he said. "That priest a yours is comin to save you. Climbin the hillside even as we speak."

She looked up.

"Oh," he said. "So that's how it is?"

She looked him straight in the eyes.

His eyes — glossy like wet stones.

"I know you," she said. "Know your type. You ain't jus crazy. You're sick."

"Darlin," he said. "We all sick."

"No," she said. "Not like that."

"Like what then?"

"Like you're diseased," she said. "Like mange. Like you got mange on your soul. You scratch at it. You pick. But you ain't never get rid a it. It's part a you. It's who you is. And you can't never escape. No matter how you try."

"Okay," he said. "That's enough."

She looked at him intently.

"I know you," she said. "I knowed it by your eyes. They're black. Nothin behind them but dark. And yet—that ain't you neither."

"Okay," he said. "I said enough."

"No," she said. "That ain't you. You ain't nothin but a boy. A sick boy. A scared boy. And all you want is to be set free. But you just can't grab it."

"You shut your mouth," he said.

Suddenly, she reached out to touch him.

"Go on," she said. "Call me mama."

He recoiled in disgust.

"That's a mistake," he said. "I'm goin to make you regret it."

Outside, the boy stood and listened. He had heard their conversation and thought about going in. But what he heard next was just too horrible. He couldn't bear it. He walked to the hillside, put his hands on his knees, and he began heaving until he threw up.

❦

The rain had stopped on that summer night in 1850 and the clouds had broken up revealing the starcrested firmament, the million tiny fires that led wanderers to war and home and the places in between. Ignacio and the bounty hunter had emerged from their negotiations, pointed their guns at the inmate outside, and forced him right back into the chains from which he had just been freed.

"But I thought we was friends," he said to Ignacio.

"I know you did," Ignacio said.

"I showed you my toe."

"Come on," Ignacio said. "Let's get movin."

"I told you how I got it."

"Go on," Ignacio said. "We ain't got all night."

"I's trusted you," the inmate said. "You gave me your word. Said I'd be a free man. Ain't that mean nothin?"

"No," Ignacio said. "It don't."

The inmate looked from one man to the other.

They looked down at him from their horses and peered over the barrels of their guns.

The inmate sat down in the dirt.

"No," he said. "You shoot me here. I ain't goin nowhere in these chains."

The bounty hunter got down from his horse and hit the inmate in the head with the butt end of his shotgun.

"We ain't askin."

The blow knocked the inmate over and when he sat up, he was dazed and bleeding crimson blood.

"This how it's goin to be?" he said to Ignacio.

"This how it is," the bounty hunter replied.

The inmate looked Ignacio in the eyes.

Ignacio looked away.

The inmate nodded and picked up the chains.

"Now there's a good negro," the bounty hunter said. "We ain't need no fuss."

"Okay," the inmate said. "Okay."

Then he turned to Ignacio.

"But I want you to know somethin. I want you to remember. I ain't forgive you. No matter how much you regret it. No matter how many nights you spend on your knees repentin. I know what it's like to wants forgiveness. I know what it's like to need it. How it eat at you. Gnaws at your soul. And I ain't forgive you. Not now. Not never."

The bounty hunter laughed but Ignacio didn't. His horse stirred and he calmed it. Then the inmate climbed onto the back of the horse and they rode on in silence.

When they reached their destination, the moon was bright overhead. They rode through a small town on the coast north of Brownsville. It was before dawn and the streets were empty. The air was cool and a breeze came in off the gulf. There were crickets chirping in the wood and bats darting through the night sky. They rode north up a steep hill and came to a stop at an old Methodist church. They tied their horses to a post out front and walked around back.

"What's this?" the bounty hunter said.

"What's it look like?" Ignacio said.

"Look like a churchyard to me," the inmate said.

"I know what it is and what it ain't," the bounty hunter said. "Why we here?"

"You want your money?" Ignacio said.

The bounty hunter grunted.

"Boy," Ignacio said. "Grab one a them shovels and follow me."

The inmate picked up a shovel from a newly planted grave and the three men walked through the churchyard in silence. Then Ignacio came to a stop in front of an old, worn stone. It was cut in the shape of a cross and it was covered in green and white lichen. Ignacio bowed his head and removed his hat.

"M. Xavier Clem," the bounty hunter read. "1783 to 1831."

"Who that?" the inmate said.

"This?" the bounty hunter said. "If I'm not mistaken, this here's the man who gave our friend that mud-ugly scar."

The inmate looked at his fellow prisoner's face.

"Well fuck," he said. "This the old boy who cut you up?"

Ignacio nodded.

"1831?" the inmate said. "You must a jus been a kid."
Ignacio nodded again.

"How'd he end up in this grave?"
Ignacio returned his hat to his head.

"Dig," he said.

"What?" the inmate said.

"Dig," Ignacio said. "Until you hit wood."

❦

Ignacio decided that it would be better to leave his colt behind and to make the climb on foot. The rain was coming down hard and the hill was steep and wet. The horse was fast but less agile and it made for a bigger target. What's more, he would need to take his time if he was going to follow the boy's track. He checked his pistol and his carbine, put his knife in his boot, his pistol in his belt, and slung his club over his shoulder. He cupped his hands and collected some water that was falling from the sky above. It was cool and clear. He raised his hands to his lips and drank it down. Then he let out a low sigh and coughed and spit. He patted his horse twice on the nose and began the long climb up the side of the hill not knowing what he was expecting to find.

The hillside was lined with burnt, yellow grass and thorny shrubs. Tough desert roots clutched at the dry rock and the rain turned the dust to mud. There was no path to follow, no clearing to guide the way. The mines had been abandoned for a half decade or more and the hill was overgrown with thistles and weeds. Ignacio followed the markings left by the boy, some bent grass here, a half a footprint there. He walked slowly, cautiously, knowing that each step increased the danger and that a single misstep might mean death.

A little over halfway up the hill, he found the body of a dead bird. It had been split in two by a rifle shot and its blood stained the damp desert earth. He bent down and picked up the disfigured carcass. It was warm to the touch, not dead more than an hour. Suddenly, he was overcome by an odd, swooning sensation. This bird, torn in two, with blood in its eye. A subtle, delicate beauty. So perfect. Its life now gone. Cold and perfect still. Other birds—sparrows and flycatchers, the ovenbird, the thrush. There was a quiet beauty to the world. A world made perfect and more imperfect each day. And always this blood in the eye. No escaping this blood in the eye. Gray clouds seemed to gather overhead. The world, both beautiful and menacing. And nothing for us to do.

He glanced up and saw a rocky ledge overlooking the plains. He knew he was being watched from the hills above and from above the hills. There, he thought. That's where I'll find them. On that ledge. He kicked a stone over with his foot, placed the bird in the hollow beneath, covered it with some dirt, and continued his climb upwards. As he approached, he felt a sick feeling in his gut and knew that something was wrong. He stopped and stood very still. The wind rustled the brush and the rain pattered off the rocks. There was a flash of lightning in the distance and the low groan of thunder rumbled through the hills. He waited. Listened. Another flash and more thunder. He bent down and picked up an empty cartridge shell lying on the damp sod at his feet. He put it in his pocket and looked from side to side.

"You're waitin," he said. "But where?"

He could feel the man's black eyes on him like the eyes of god and he thought of what Brother Markel had said about the lord—always here, always watching. He scanned the hillside above and the slope below but saw no one. Then he heard a sound like muffled cries. He peered up over the ledge and saw a black hollow cut out of the rock. It was a cave. An opening that led to one of the old mineshafts.

He held his carbine out in front of him and slowly approached. As he did, the cries grew louder and more awful. They sounded like the whines of a dying animal. He stood outside and his heart began to race. He felt it knock hard against his ribs and he could not slow his breathing. Then he entered the cave and squinted as his eyes adjusted to the dark. The cries echoed off the walls and filled his ears and he saw the tools and the firelight and the scene laid out before him. He dropped his gun to the ground, fell to his knees, and began to heave.

❧❦❧

"Hey, boy," the man said. "You know what day it is?"

The altar boy did not answer.

"Today," the man said. "What day is this?"

The boy did not look up.

"Good Friday," the man said.

The wind blew through the brush.

"Good Friday. What's that?"

The rain beat down on the rocks below and the rumble of thunder reverberated in the distance.

"What happened on Good Friday?" the man said. "You know?"

The boy looked across to the neighboring hillside. He fixed his eyes on the ledge and on the hollow in the rock. Then he looked away.

"Boy," the man said. "Come here."

The boy did not move.

"Come here," the man said. "You know I ain't askin."

The boy walked over.

"Closer," the man said and he patted his knee. "Right here on my lap."

The boy sat on the man's lap.

"Today," the man said, "is the day a the crucifixion."

The boy cringed at the word.

"You know what that means?" the man said. "Crucifixion?"

The boy looked down.

The man ran his fingers through the boy's hair.

The boy did not move.

"Now listen close," the man said. "I'm a teach you somethin."

"I know what it means," the boy said.

The man smiled.

"Good boy," he said. "What's it mean?"

The boy did not respond.

"Go on," the man said. "Don't be shy."

The boy was silent still.

"You know how he dies?" the man said. "The crucified one?"

The boy began to shake.

"Not from the wounds," the man said. "No. That'd be too easy. Too quick. You see the point a crucifixion is to make him suffer. To make it last. The point is to force him to feel his death as long and as deep as any man ever could."

The boy trembled.

"Funny when you think about it. What kind a creature wants to see that much sufferin? What kind a creature wants to cause that amount a pain?"

The boy wiped his nose.

"Now don't get me wrong," the man said. "The beast'll kill you. He'll kill you dead and he won't think nothin of it. But that's only to survive. Only cause he has to. That's only cause he wants to live. He don't revel in it. He don't enjoy himself."

He paused and thought about that and the two sat without talking, the boy on the man's lap, the man petting him tenderly, each respecting the silence of the other, neither willing to utter a word. Then the man lifted the boy's chin and looked straight down into his eyes.

"Asphyxiation," he said.

The boy looked at him intently, not knowing how to respond.

"Asphyxiation," the man said. "You know what that is?"

The boy felt uneasy and he tried to look away.

"Asphyxiation," the man said and he wrapped his hands around the boy's throat, holding his head in place.

The boy stared up into his dark, yellow eyes.

"Asphyxiation. It's what kills him, hangin there on that cross."

The boy struggled but the man only tightened his grip.

"It's when you can't breathe," the man said. "When you choke yourself to death."

And the man squeezed.

The boy began flailing his arms, trying to break free.

The man stood and lifted him off of the ground. He held him up by the neck and the boy pulled at his hands but he could not wrench them loose.

"Now why do you think that is?" the man said. "Why do you think it causes asphyxiation?"

The boy's eyes rolled back in his head.

The man lowered him back to the ground and released his grip.

The boy fell, coughing, and he heaved and rubbed his throat.

The man walked to the hillside and looked over at the ledge and at the hollow in the rock.

"It's cause he's got his arms stretched out over his head," he said with his back to the boy. "They're what hold him to the wood. And all that weight pulls on his arms. His whole body. So they disjoint. He has to keep liftin himself and holdin up all that weight. But he ain't strong enough to do it. He tries and he

120

tries but he ain't strong enough. And he begins to feel like he's bein crushed. Like someone's pressin in on his ribs. And he can't breathe and he tries and he tries. He wants to cry out but instead he just chokes and sucks at the air."

The boy wheezed and struggled to catch his breath.

"That's when he knows what he's known all along. That he was made to die here alone. And can't no one save him."

The boy rubbed his throat and coughed. Then he looked up at the man.

"That was a mistake," he said.

The man turned.

The boy stood and spat.

"You should a killed me."

❦

Her body was soft and womanly. She had smooth, white skin, small, curved breasts, round hips, and a plump belly that sloped gently to her thighs. Her hair was long and curled. Her toes small and white. She had thin, pale lips and full almond-shaped eyes. Her eyebrows were light but darker than her hair and her forehead creased in the middle. Her nose was small and thin. Her nostrils flared when she cried. She wore a wreath of lilies in her hair and nothing on her naked, white flesh. Her thighs pressed together in the shape of a V. Her back arched forward off the wood. Her arms stretched out over her head. Driven through her wrists were old, rusted nails. And through her feet—a cold, metal spike. They held her in place, fixed to the wooden ties. She might have looked beautiful hanging there, like a Renaissance painting. Except she kept coughing and gasping for air and she had been crucified.

HOLY SATURDAY ✿

Deep in the hollow of the rock, Brother Markel the Seer lay facedown prostrate before the ornate gold cross. The fire had burned itself out. The candles had dwindled to nothing. The cave was as black as the world inhabited by the sightless old monk. There was no light and no sound. Nothing to see or to be seen. No movement and Markel did not move. He lay there motionless, like a dead man shot through the back to water the dry sod. His body was stiff, his face pressed down into the earth, his arms stretched out before him toward the altar. He was clothed in a simple brown tunic. His feet were dirty and bare. His hands dry. His teeth ground together, clenched tight to the jaw. The blood on his back had clotted and it scabbed and stuck to his cloak. His fingers were withered and old with cracked yellow nails and hairless gray spots. His breathing was short. He took quick, shallow breaths in and out and wheezed and sucked at the air.

He had been lying on the ground since collapsing in a fit of tremors two days before. At first, he was unconscious. But when he awoke, he simply rolled over onto his stomach and lay there. He did not move or stir. He did not sleep or cough or blink. He just stared down at the dry dirt beneath his nose, at the nothing, the filth and the dark.

Yet, blind as he was, still the old monk could see. He could see the events of the past week—the murders, the scalpings, the fire, the blood. He could see months and years and centuries gone by, the vast and growing multitude undone by the blackness of death. He could see dry bones, bloodless flesh and fleshless faces. He fixed his gaze to the east and saw nothing but stone and ash and a dry and dusty wind. He looked to the west and saw rotting entrails that once were a man, faceless mounds that once were an army, a barren desert that once was the world. He saw it all—time past and time future, cities rising and falling, plagues and wars and famines, great storms and the scorched desert earth, slavery and bondage, old men begging to die, infants slaughtered before life began, disease and contagion, chains and ropes and metal bars, rapes and incest and unspeakable torments, birth and death and copulation. He saw torchlight red on sweaty faces. The grabbing, pulling, punching blows. He saw whips and clubs and instruments of torture and the cool, lipless grin of the one who held them. And he saw blood. Blood that stains hands and houses. Blood that spills and muddies the ground. Blood that runs like rivers to the sea. That reddens the land and darkens the earth. Blood that cries out for vengeance.

He saw it all, tomorrow and every tomorrow, yesterday and each day before it, the whole history of the world mysteriously summed up and seen all at once, gathered before him in the light of a single, blue flame.

"Kyrie eleison," he said. "Christe eleison."

He fixed his eyes on that flame. A flame bluer than his eyes and more opaque. He had seen it before, many times, and had come to cherish it so dearly that he felt it was more a part of him than was his name. The flame, he thought, is this poor old monk. But he ain't the flame. He ain't make it. He ain't bring it to be. He ain't nothin but a witness. A witness to the light. A witness to the flame that enters his soul and makes him all he is. And though he was blind and could not see, still he saw the flame. A flame not imagined, not dreamed up, but there, truly there, as present to him as were his bones. No matter how black and dead his eyes, still he saw the light. A single flame, glowing in the dark. A true presence. A perpetual light.

"Kyrie eleison," he said. "Christe eleison."

The flame grew brighter.

"Kyrie eleison. Christe eleison."

It grew brighter still.

"Kyrie eleison. Christe eleison."

The walls ignited and fire spread from one wall to the next. The candles spontaneously lit and the altar was encircled in flames, dancing and smoking and licking the air. Markel pushed himself up off the ground. He could see more clearly than ever and he watched as the flames rose and surrounded him. The walls were engulfed. Fire spread across the ceiling and glowing embers fell like stars to the floor. He stood in the middle of a blazing inferno, feet hot and dancing on the coals. The fire whirled and he could see himself in the flames. He was sweating and panting and he stripped naked and threw his cloak into the blaze. It burnt blue and green and red as blood.

Markel began dancing wildly. He clapped and cheered and sang out in joy. He spun and spun and his eyes flashed blue and his feet charred black and he waved his hands in the air.

"He alive!" he shouted. "Hallelujah, he alive!"

He danced and spun and kicked his feet.

"He alive!" he said. "Forever and ever!"

The flames burned all around him and he reached out and touched them but they did not burn his flesh.

"Forever and ever and he won't never die!"

He stomped his feet on the embers and beat his fists on his chest and he danced in jubilant celebration. His whole body was atremble and he began to shake. He was filled with agony and ecstasy and he wept and cried out.

"He alive! He alive! He won't never die!"

And he fell to the ground shaking, let out a terrible groan, and died on the spot.

❧✦❧

Maryellen would spend the next three weeks wrapped in bandages, coming in and out of consciousness, tossing and turning on a small cot in the nearby orphanage. There, she would be nursed back to health by the desert nuns who helped Ignacio care for the lost and abandoned children of the Arizona territory. The nuns' pilgrimage to the mission in Tucson had spared them the carnage inflicted upon the town. They had returned to find their home intact and Maryellen in their care. She stayed with them for over six months, resting and healing and learning to pray. On Saturdays, the sisters would dress her in a simple, blue dress and carry her to the chapel where a priest from another parish would come to offer the mass. He would walk down the center aisle to where she lay sprawled out on her cot. Then he would bend down, kiss her forehead, and place the host on her tongue. She would receive it with tears but she would not speak. Not to anyone. Not the nuns. Not the priest. Not the orphans. Not even to her god.

During her six-month recovery, Maryellen refused to sleep alone. Each night, one of the sisters would climb into her bed and hold her while she cried and shook and screamed in terror. The nuns washed her and fed her and tended her wounds. They read to her from the gospels or from the lives of the saints and she would gaze off at nothing and pretend not to listen. But she always listened. Sometimes she would close her eyes and imagine that she was dead. She wondered what it felt like to be dead—whether dying hurt more than living or whether both hurt the same—and she thought about how there was one way to find out.

It would take her the better part of three months to put weight on her feet and even longer to stand without assistance. After five months, she was able to walk with a crutch and after six she could sleep through the night without waking. Sometimes she would be overcome by coughing fits that would last for hours and she would hack and cough and suck at the air. Her lungs would fill with fluid and she would feel like she was choking and drowning all at once. It was during one such fit that a nun had given her an old rosary and told her that any time she felt like she was losing control all she had to do was squeeze its wooden beads and remember that her life was not her own and that she had control over nothing. She listened to that nun and did as she was told and it seemed to help so she carried the rosary with her and used it from time to time.

Her stay with the sisters would prove formative. Less than a year after being rescued from the cave, Maryellen would join their order, changing her name to Sister Maria de la Soledad and taking her vows on Candlemas 1862. She would dedicate herself to a life of poverty, spending her nights sleeping out on the desert rocks rather than on a cot or bed in the orphanage. The children would fall in love with her and they would follow wherever she'd go. Some would ask how she got such awful scars and she would say that she had had them for most of her life and they would say that that didn't explain how she got them and she would smile and say yes, it did.

The younger nuns would grow jealous of her. They would become annoyed with her fondness for the children and suspicious of the strictness with which she kept the rule. They would wait until she had left for the day and would call her "Maria de la Stigmata." They would say that her wounds had special healing powers and would joke about her being the chosen bride of Christ. Then they would laugh and say that she was the secret mistress of a heretic priest, a Magdala without the contrite heart, a godless, faithless, contemptible whore. They would spit on the ground and say that Christ would never condescend for such an ugly bride and they would crush small berries in the palms of their hands and pretend that they too had her wounds. Their mother superior would hear of their contempt and she would discipline them harshly and Maryellen knew all but she ignored them and pretended she knew nothing.

She would spend most of her days alone, wandering the hillside in silent prayer. She would walk barefoot across the scorched desert earth, fasting and praying and mortifying her flesh. The jagged stones would cut the bottoms of her feet and her wounds would reopen and she would let them bleed and the blood would stain the dry ground. Then she would wash her feet in a small brook, feed on berries and the roots of wild plants, kneel and pray and cry out to god. She would be very silent and very still and would wait and listen. But god would not answer and she would weep bitterly and wonder whether he had anything to say or whether silence was all he could muster.

At night, she would dream of Ignacio. She would see him standing before her, smoking in his black cassock or kneeling by the old Spanish altar dressed in vestments of crimson and gold. His face was no longer scarred but his hands were red and covered in blood. He did not speak. He just stood and stared or knelt and prayed.

One night, she had the most vivid, the most real of dreams. And after that, she never dreamt of him again. He stood at a distance in a long, white robe and there was a leafy crown in his hair and a flaming torch in his hand. The two of them were in the desert and it was the break of day and she called to him but he did not answer. Instead, he turned and ran east toward the rising sun. As the first rays of dawn spread like fingers across the land and the sun broke red and gold over the plains, he lifted his torch high in the air and sun and flame united as a single fiery incandescence. They came together as one burning light, radiating through the heavens and the earth. She chased him and chased him and drew closer but she could not reach him. Instead, the flaming sun grew larger and larger and all was consumed in a white abyss the depths of which she could not understand. The light entered her as she entered it and she cried out in agony and ecstasy but her cries were silent and nobody heard. She awoke with a start and found herself lying face down on the rocky desert earth. It was dawn and the sun was just rising over the ridge. She stood, dusted her feet, and walked east toward the break of day, sensing that her hour had finally come. And though she did not know what that meant, she knew that her destination was fixed and that no one would ever hear from her again.

❧❧❧

Ignacio stayed with her at the orphanage until after midnight, holding her, rocking her, kissing her wounds. Then he left for good. He set out on horseback knowing in his heart that his decision to return to the mines meant that he would never see her again. His hour had come. And while he did not know what would what happen, he knew he would not return. He knew he would never see her, hold her, touch her again. If he lived, he would be unable to face her having done the one thing he swore he would not do. And if he died—well, what forgiveness could there be if he died?

Yet even knowing this, still he felt ready to die. He felt ready and he felt an odd sort of calm about his readiness. It was as if he had no say in the matter. As if the choice was not his. As if it was up to someone else and that someone had nothing left to decide. The only thing for him to do was wait and see how it landed. My life, he thought, is not my own and I control nothing. He was filled with an inexplicable certainty that his story had already been written, his life already lived, his thoughts and feelings and actions already thought and felt and acted out. All of them done before. All completed. All part of the drama of an existence always already pointing to one end and one end alone. He did not know what that end was. He did not know if he would kill or if he would be killed. But it did not matter. Whatever was going to happen was going to happen as it was meant to happen from the start. However this was going to end, it was going to end well. He felt certain of that. As if he knew because he had always known. As if he knew because he had already lived. And more than once. Time and again.

All of this came as a relief. He felt as if he could finally let himself go. As if he were in possession of some impossible good news that changed everything and made everything what it was. But more than that, he was filled with a strange, swooning sensation. A feeling of powerlessness. A feeling of loss. As if he were suspended out over the void and could be dropped at any moment. And the decision was not his to make.

He sighed and gripped the mane of his colt. Then he dug his heels deep into its boney ribs and raced toward the town at a gallop. The rain had stopped and the clouds parted overhead revealing a brilliant black sky dotted white with stars. The moon hung low on the horizon, veiled behind a violet haze. It cast dark shadows across the land like the shadows cast at the break of day. He urged his horse on through the rubble that once had been his home, through the blood, through the embers, through the dirt and brush and barren plains. He rode over the dry desert rocks, over the dying roots, through the dark, desert valley, across the flatlands and the sunburnt earth.

When he reached the foot of the hill, he felt his calm leave him and his heart was filled with nothing but hardness and a cold, bitter hate. The events of the past week were enough to turn the most decent of men cruel and the horror of that night was more than any man should have to bear. He had pushed it, as best as he could, from his mind. But now, as he returned to the place of the crime, a savage, cutting meanness bit down into his soul and it weighed on him like a millstone hung heavy round his neck. His face hardened into a scowl and he gritted his teeth. He had aged a decade in a day and he looked hard and mean. He spat and dug his feet into the sides of his horse and when it did not run fast enough, he beat his fists down on its neck. It screamed and charged headlong into the night and he urged it faster and faster up the side of the ridge.

The climb was steep and Ignacio clung to the mane of his horse. He charged up the hill like a crusader charging at a moorish castle. Suddenly a flash of white burst out from the darkness above and before he heard the pop of the gun, his colt had collapsed beneath him and he had been thrown to the muddy earth. He landed and the horse cried and kicked and crimson blood poured from its breast. It snorted and tried to stand but it staggered and another shot rang out. Ignacio heard the whizz of the bullet and there was a loud snap as it lodged itself in the horse's brain. A spurt of blood sprayed into the air and the horse was dead before it hit the ground.

Ignacio grabbed his carbine from the dirt and crawled quickly to a nearby stone. He ducked down behind it and his heart began to race. He felt it knock hard against his ribs and he could not slow his breathing. Another blast and he heard the bullet bounce off the rock behind him. Then another, this time closer. And another, closer still.

"Father," the man called.

He was walking slowly down the hillside with his rifle at his waist and his finger on the trigger.

"Father," he said. "I don't believe."

He pulled the trigger and another shot rang out.

"I don't believe," he said. "It ain't true."

Ignacio raised the barrel of his carbine over the stone and fired blindly.

The man shot back and Ignacio heard the bullet fly past.

"I don't believe you done it," he said. "Don't believe you could."

The man walked right around the stone and pressed the barrel of his gun against the face of the cowering priest.

Ignacio looked up.

"You ain't no Joseph of Arimathea."

❧❦❧

"Alright. Time to get up."

The bounty hunter cocked one eye open and looked at the owner of the plantation standing before him, dressed to the hilt in military regalia, a few red whiskers sprouting from his boyish chin. It was a bright summer morning in 1850 and, after a couple of weeks on horseback—traveling with his prisoner from Texas to Mississippi—the bounty hunter had been looking forward to a full night's rest.

"Slept long enough," said the owner.

"Now what in the hell is this?" the bounty hunter said.

"Got something to show you," the owner said.

"Where'd you get that uniform?" the bounty hunter said.

"It's mine," the owner said.

"Like hell it is," the bounty hunter said. "You ain't know a war from a whistle stop."

"I seen my share a action," the owner said. "It's violence that run through these veins."

"It belongs to your pa," the bounty hunter said. "Seen that portrait a him hangin in the main hall."

The owner looked at the ground.

The bounty hunter examined him.

Hair parted in the middle, shoulders slumped forward, long, thin arms hanging at his sides—he was more a mouth than a man. He was a boy playing dress-up, trying to be what he took a man to be.

"Ain't no shame in it," the bounty hunter said. "No man's life's his own."

"How's that?" the owner said.

"Belong to the one who raised him," the bounty hunter said. "Each a us has to wrestle with the shadow a that ghost."

"It's his," the owner said begrudgingly. "But I'll ride out in it one day too."

"Don't doubt you will," the bounty hunter said. "Don't doubt it for a minute."

"There'll be war enough," the owner said. "Glory and battle and the taste a blood."

The bounty hunter grunted.

"And if them negro-lovers up north keep it up, I'll have my portrait hangin in that hall real soon."

"Where'd he fight?" the bounty hunter said. "Your old man?"

"Held the line in 12," the owner said. "And again in Texas. That's where we lost him, god rest his soul."

"Sorry to hear it," the bounty hunter said.

The owner nodded.

"He a good fighter?" the bounty hunter said.

"Good ain't the half of it," the owner said. "Couldn't be beat."

"Well, okay then," the bounty hunter said and he closed his eyes.

The boyish man looked at him in disbelief. His

face turned as red as his thin, red beard. His eyes narrowed and he wrinkled his freckle-covered forehead.

"Hey," he said.

"Hey what?" the bounty hunter said.

"Get up," the owner said.

"No," the bounty hunter said.

"Get up," the owner said.

The bounty hunter opened his eyes and looked at him.

"I got somethin to show you," the owner said. "Hangin in the shed out back."

"Now you listen here," the bounty hunter said. "I ain't want a stay on this god-cursed plantation in the first place. I'd a been happy leavin last night. You're the one who insisted."

"I got somethin to show you," the owner said.

"Can't a man get no goddamn sleep?"

"No," the owner said. "He can't."

The bounty hunter grunted. He swung his big legs to the edge of the bed and sat up. He was dressed in his host's long underwear and he was sleeping in the guesthouse.

"Now there's a good fella," the owner said.

"I ain't havin none of it," the bounty hunter said. "Ain't in the mood."

"You come with me," the owner said. "I ain't paid you yet."

The bounty hunter looked at him.

"Don't make me take what's mine," he said.

"I'll have the sheriff after you before you can pull on them boots," the owner said.

"And if I put a bullet right between that sheriff's eyes?" the bounty hunter said.

"It's a thing to do," the owner said. "But you won't get far. Got family from here to California. We'll track you down."

"Make it four hundred," the bounty hunter said.

"How's that?" the owner said.

"For the trouble," the bounty hunter said. "Don't make like you ain't got it."

The young man rubbed his chin.

"Tell you what," he said. "Get up, come with me, see what I got to show you. I'll give you three-fifty and a partin gift for the road."

The bounty hunter stooped his head and spat right there on the wood floor.

"Three-fifty?" he said.

"Three-fifty," the owner said. "Now get dressed. I'll meet you in the main hall."

When the bounty hunter descended the stairs, he was met by the young man and his house slave Garrison.

"Goodday, sir," Garrison said. "Hope the room was to yar likin."

The bounty hunter looked at him.

He had old, honest eyes that seemed to take life for what it was.

The bounty hunter looked away.

"Come," the owner said. "Follow me."

The bounty hunter followed and Garrison went upstairs to change the linens.

Outside there was singing in the fields and the sound of plows in the dirt. It was a humid Mississippi morning and a low, moist haze hung in the air. The sky was red and the light reflected off the mist forcing the bounty hunter to squint. There were birds chirping in the wood and there was a lone thrush calling out to listeners unknown. The bounty hunter spat on the grassy earth and the young man led him through the fields to an old, dilapidated shed.

As the men approached, they could hear the sound of flies nesting and biting and beating their wings. And there was a groaning like the groans of a dying pig coming from within.

"Here," the owner said and he handed the bounty hunter a small parcel.

"What's this?" the bounty hunter said.

"Open it."

The bounty hunter looked at him.

"Go on," the owner said. "Open it."

The groaning continued and it sounded wretched and pathetic.

"It's for you. Open it."

The bounty hunter unwrapped the wax paper and looked at what was inside.

"What is it?" he said.

Folded up in the package was a ball of black flesh, small and bloody.

The young man pushed open the door of the shed.

Inside it was hot and damp and the bounty hunter squinted as his eyes adjusted to the dark. Then he saw what the young man had done, what he had been so eager to show. He saw the inmate in chains, hands cuffed, hanging from the rafters. He saw his wounds and the blood and he thought he might be sick.

"Christ," he said. "Jesus Christ."

"It's his toe," the owner said.

"Jesus Christ."

"It's his little toe."

❧❀❧

"Hey, boy," the man said. "Come here."

The altar boy walked over.

"You're a good boy," the man said. "I like you."

"Thank you," the boy said.

"Thank you what?" the man said.

"Thank you, pa," the boy said.

"There it is," the man said and he grinned. "That's a good boy."

The boy nodded.

"Come here," the man said. "Closer."

135

The boy walked closer.

"Right here," the man said. "On my lap."

The boy sat down on the man's lap.

"That's a good boy," the man said and he stroked his hair.

The boy did not move.

"You're a good boy," the man said. "Real good."

The boy stared off blankly.

There was a long silence and the man continued to rub his hand through the boy's hair.

"Hey, pa," the boy said.

"Yes?" the man said.

"Tell me a story," the boy said.

"A story?" the man said. "What kind a story you want to hear?"

"I don't know," the boy said. "A good one."

"A good one?" the man said. "What's makes a story good?"

"I don't know," the boy said.

"You and me both," the man said.

"Tell me a story about good guys and bad guys," the boy said. "A story that ain't true."

"Now why'd you want to go and hear a thing like that?"

"I don't know," the boy said. "It's good. At least, it can be."

The man smiled.

"Alright," he said. "If it's what you want."

"It is, pa," the boy said. "It's what I want."

"Alright," the man said. "How's this? There once was a wise and humble man who lived all by himself in the wilderness."

"Why'd he do that?" the boy said.

"Well," the man said. "He wasn't exactly an ordinary man. He was a monk, a hermit, a mystic a sorts. By the world's estimation, he was a fool. And so he was. Give up his land and his wife and his livin to go

136

into the wild and commit himself to the ways a the almighty. He lived for his god and for nothin else."

"But why?" the boy said. "Why'd he do it?"

"Don't ask why," the man said. "It jus was."

The boy nodded as if he understood.

"One day," the man said, "this wise and holy monk is out tendin the land. Just like the first man. Just like the last man still to come. He tends it cause it's what he's good at. What he was made to do. Tends it mornin and night. Waters it, plows it, sows the seeds. And he loves to tend. Lives for it. Expects to tend til the day he becomes like the earth and there's someone else to tend the sod that once was his soul. But that ain't what happens. Not at all."

"What happens?" the boy said.

"He hears a noise," the man said. "Like horses through the wood. Then he sees it—the royal parade."

"What's that?" the boy said.

"It's the king," the man said. "And all his company too. Come ridin through the forest on horseback just to find this old monk."

"How come?" the boy said.

"The king's rich," the man said. "And powerful. He can have and do anythin he wants. He has women and wine and when he feels restless, he starts wars and goes off to battle. He throws decadent balls and has whores and court jesters to beat and abuse for his pleasure. He sleeps on a bed a satin in a room with a fire and his belly full a rum. But for all that, he ain't happy. Not a bit. And with each passin day, he grows more miserable still."

The man ran his hand through the boy's hair.

The boy listened intently.

"The king's come for one reason and one reason alone. He wants to be happy. And he thinks this monk can show him how. So he rides up with his royal procession—knights and guards and ladies in the back. He dismounts and approaches the old monk. 'Good sir,' he says. 'I heard much a you. Your legend spreads like pestilence through the countryside.' The monk does not look up. He just keeps tendin the land. 'I've come,' says the king, 'to learn your ways. Teach me your secret wisdom and I'll forever be in your debt.' But the monk keeps tendin. 'Do you know,' says the king, 'that I'm the ruler a this land? The ground you work belongs to me.' The monk says not a word. 'Give me that spade,' says the king and he grabs a hold of it. 'You do as I say.' The monk stops and looks him straight in the eyes. He's silent but he looks. 'Will you teach me?' says the king. The monk does not answer. Instead he raises his hand high and strikes him on the head.

"That's when the knights and guards unsheathe their swords. They jump down from their horses ready to spill blood. But the king drops to his knees, stunned and weeping. He kisses the ground at the monk's feet and cries out. 'Sir,' he says. 'You're a wise and holy man. Teach and I will obey. Guide and I will follow. I want nothin more than to do your pleasure.' The monk picks up his spade and he turns and walks off into the wood. The king rises to his feet. He sends his procession away and chases after him."

"Say, pa," the boy said.

"Yes?" the man said.

"What's it mean?" the boy said.

"Don't ask what it means," the man said. "Jus listen."

"Okay," the boy said.

"The king," the man said, "spent the night on the ground outside the monk's hut. And the next night. And the night after that. The monk said not a word. He went about his business as if the king wasn't even there. He woke at dawn and knelt and prayed. He worked the land and fed on berries and dry grass. He drank honey from a nest a bees and washed himself in a nearby brook. And the king followed everywhere he went. He studied him. He shadowed him. He shadowed his every move. If the monk tended, the king tended. If he ate, he ate. If he prayed, he prayed. If he sat, he sat. And when he was silent, the king said nothin at all. Life went on this way for weeks. And weeks turned to months. And the king found contentment in the forest. And his life took on a new and noble meanin. And he acquired much wisdom."

The boy coughed.

The man rubbed the boy's hair.

The boy leaned his head against the man's chest.

"One day," the man said, "when the two were out workin the land, the monk turns and looks at the king. 'Tell me,' he says. 'What have you learned?' The king looks at him in disbelief—stunned to hear the old hermit's voice. It's gentle like the voice of a woman. But his words are harsh like a general at war. 'Tell me,' the monk says. 'You've been here long enough.' But the king doesn't know how to answer. He stammers and struggles and tries to gather his words. 'I've learned,' he says, 'that strength comes not from power. That wisdom ain't a this world. That happiness means givin away. That sacrifice is the heart a love.' 'No,' says the monk. 'Try again.' 'I've learned,' the king says, 'that you can't learn. That unlearnin is the only way. That truth hides in the dark of unknowin.' 'No,' says the monk. 'Try again.' 'I've learned,' says the king, 'that silence is the voice a god. That mystery is his only word. That we know him by his absence. That we find him when he's not there.' 'No,' says the monk. 'Not at all.'

"The king does not know what this means. He clenches his jaw and his eyes start to water. 'What then?' says he. 'What good is any of it?' 'What then?' says the monk. 'What good?' The king grabs a hold a the spade and he swings it wildly. He stands over the monk teaming with anger and with hate. The monk looks up at him and he smiles. 'There it is,' he says. 'That's it. Now you see it's come to this.'

"The next day, a group a knights—the king's most loyal and lovin compatriots—set out to find their lost friend. It's been months and they're ready to have him home. The court's been lonesome without him. They come to the place where they saw him last but he ain't there. The clearin is empty. So they go on deeper into the wood, followin the sounds and the signs a the forest. Soon they stumble upon the hut where the old monk lives. There he is, tendin the land with his spade. But no sign a their king. No sign a the friend they left behind. Then one a them points. 'Look,' says he. 'Up there on that branch.'

"And there, stretched out, is the bloody skin. The scalp of a man dryin in the sun."

❦

After the altar boy had finished pulling the scalp from Ignacio's head, the man had him help carry the chained and mutilated body up the side of the ridge to the cave where Maryellen had been crucified. The hill was steep and the boy slipped on the way up, dropping the body to the muddy ground. Ignacio grunted and he let out a low, gurgling whine. The man looked at the boy and told him not to let it happen again and the boy made sure that he did as he was told.

When they reached the ledge, it was dawn and the day was just breaking over the hillside to the east. The morning star was visible before the sun and it shined bright and illuminated the sky. The boy looked out at the quiet Arizona desert and he cursed the sun and the sky for bringing the new day.

"Let's set him down here," the man said. "And sit him up straight."

They leaned Ignacio against a rock and his body slumped over, head hanging forward in his lap.

"Here," the man said. "Feed him this."

He handed the boy the dry roots of a plant.

The boy opened Ignacio's mouth and blood poured out onto his hands. He placed the roots under the dying priest's tongue and he walked away.

"Now," the man said, "we wait."

The boy walked to the side of the ledge and sat with his back to the man and his knees pulled tight to his chest. He lowered his head and closed his eyes and he rocked himself back and forth.

The man paced about, rubbing his hands and talking to himself in short, inaudible sentences. At times, he would lose his temper and yell at himself in an outburst of frustration but then he would regain his composure and pace about some more.

After a few minutes, the roots took their effect.

The priest's head shot up, eyes opened wide in terror.

"Good mornin," the man said and he rushed to his side. "Try not to move. It'll only make things worse."

Ignacio looked from the man to the boy and back again. He was bound hand and foot and his torso was wrapped in thick metal chains. He coughed and felt a rush of blood go to his head.

"I know it's hard to believe," the man said, "that it came to this. But you have to see. There ain't no other way. This is our fate. Our destiny."

Ignacio blinked and tears of blood ran from his eyes.

"It was always goin to end like this, father. I ain't choose it. You ain't choose it neither. It's been written in the stars."

Ignacio looked over at the boy.

The boy was still.

"Please," Ignacio managed to say. "Don't hurt..."
But his words trailed off.

"The boy?" the man said. "I ain't goin to hurt him. I'm goin to teach him. I'm goin to set him free."

Ignacio closed his eyes.

"Tell me," the man said. "What do you think a your god now?"

Ignacio opened his eyes and looked at him.

"What do you think of a god who could create a man like me? A god who could lead you here?"

Ignacio's lips began to move but no words came out.

The man grinned. His eyes flashed as dark and as black as onyx.

"Tell me, father. Can he hear your prayers? Is that god a yours listenin to you now?"

Ignacio mumbled something inaudible.

"Tell me," the man said. "I want to hear. I want to know if you still believe."

"You ain't a man," Ignacio whispered.

"What?" the man said and he leaned in close.

"You ain't a man," Ignacio said.

The man smiled.

"I'm a wolf," he said.

"You ain't nothin but a boy," Ignacio said. "And a sad one at that."

The man grabbed the priest by the collar and his eyes flashed red.

"Where's your god?" he said. "Why's he silent?"

But Ignacio did not speak. He just looked up at him with defeat in his eyes.

The man threw the priest to the ground and gave him a kick.

"Hey, boy," he said. "Come here."

The boy did not move.

"Come here," he said.

The boy remained still.

"No matter," the man said. "The time is now."

He bent down and picked up his prisoner in his arms.

Ignacio pulled himself up, helping to lift his own weight.

The man cradled him like a child as he walked into the blackness of the cave.

Ignacio closed his eyes and bowed his head down low.

The man walked to the edge of the mineshaft. He looked down at the simple priest shaking in his arms. Then he threw him into the pit and watched as he descended down, down into the darkness never to be heard from again.

He turned and walked out into the light of the new day. And when he did, he found that he was alone. The boy was gone and he had taken Ignacio's guns.

"You believe in god, sister?"

"I believe in sufferin," she said. "In bein crushed."

"What's that mean?" the medic said and he gave her a straight look.

The nun did not respond.

"Today's supposed to be a big day for you," the medic said. "The day a rebirth. The day a new life."

"That's every day," Maryellen said.

"Is that right?"

"I say it is."

"Well, okay then," the medic said and he spat.

The two walked on in silence through the fields. It was a warm, hazy day at the end of March and it had rained the night before, making the ground damp and the air thick. She was barefoot and the grass stuck to the bottoms of her feet and it turned her feet yellow and green. He looked at her and thought of how pretty she'd be if she didn't veil herself behind a frumpy, black habit and he wondered where she had come from and what a westerner was doing this far east. He wanted to know what made her choose to be a nun and he wondered what business a nun had doing this kind of work. He thought to ask but then thought better and he coughed and spat.

"You think it'll ever end?" the medic said. "The warrin and the bodies?"

"No," Maryellen said. "I don't."

"No," the medic said. "Me neither."

The sun was high up in the noontime sky and the stench of death and rot mixed with cold rain and hot lead burned in their noses. There were plenty to bury and they would be at it all afternoon. They would collect the tags from those who wore tags and they would send them home to wives and children, now widows and orphans, and they would return to the town and eat and sleep and do it all again the next day.

"I treated this lady once," the medic said. "Come to me with real bad pains in her neck and back and in her gut. Said she'd been havin em for weeks. Said the pains were so bad she could barely stand."

The nun held a wooden rosary in her palm and she gripped it tight making a small, cross-shaped indent in the center of her hand but the medic did not see.

"'Sit down on my table,' I said. 'Let me take a look.' So I went through the basics. Checked her pulse and her eyes and her glands. Even checked the bottoms a her feet. Checked her for cholera and diphtheria and syphilis and the sweats. Checked if she had brain fever which I'd never seen myself and only read about in books. But she looked fine to me. Couple a boils and a dead tooth but nothin that'd kill her. At least not any time soon. 'It's somethin doc,' she said. 'Every time I pass water, it burns. And I keep wakin with sweats and terrors. Feelin like somethin got a hold a my insides and it ain't never lettin go.' 'Lift your skirt,' I said. 'Let me see what we're workin with—'" He paused and smiled and expected to see the nun blush but she did not blush and he continued. "'When was the last time you had a bleed?' I said. 'Months and months,' she said. 'Well,' I said. 'There it is.' 'No,' she said. 'There it ain't.' I wasn't sure what that meant so I asked. 'I saw another doctor,' she said. 'Up north. And he helped me out. Made it real simple.'"

They came to the top of a small hill which overlooked a grassy field. The midday haze was thick and it veiled the land below in a layer of smoky gray clouds.

"'Well,' I said. 'Only one way to be sure. Spread them knees.' She gave me an awful look and she ain't move an inch. 'Come now,' I said. 'No need for niceties. I been trained.' She parted them wide

145

and I put my hand in and sure as my name is Samson that woman was with child. A big one too. She was ready to go. 'No,' she said. 'It ain't possible.' 'Well,' I said. 'It is.' 'No,' she said. 'I ain't been with no man since I was up north. Ain't even sniffed one.' 'Come now,' I said. 'No need to tell tales. I ain't your priest.'

"She took my hand in hers and looked me deep in the eye. 'Ain't a one,' she said. 'That's the truth.' I could see it was. Tell by the look she gave me. So I racked my brain and I thought and thought. 'It ain't possible,' I said. 'Ain't no one never got herself pregnant without a man somewhere in the mix.' But then it dawned on me. 'Say,' I said. 'When that doctor fixed you up, did he check if you was carryin twins?' 'Well,' she said. 'I can't rightly say.' 'Well,' I said. 'There it is. You rid yourself a the one only to keep the other. And this here's the other.' That made her cry. I put my hand on her knee and told her I understood. And to be honest, I think I did."

The two paused and looked at each.

"Well," the medic said with a sly smile. "I ain't much of a religious man—but it seem to me there's a mean sort a humor at work in that. Like someone up above havin himself a good laugh at that poor lady. What you think?"

"I don't think much," Maryellen said. "Hard enough jus to act."

The medic nodded as if he understood, but in truth he did not know what she meant.

"That must a been ten years ago if it was one," he said. "What you think happened to the other?"

"I don't know," she said.

"Prolly nothin good," he said.

"No," she said. "Prolly not."

They descended the hill in silence and came to the killing field just below the tree line. It was damp with rain and there was little drainage so the wet grass was stained red with blood. The past week had been the most violent the area had seen since the start of the war nearly three years before. There were bodies piled in heaps along the edges of the field and there were dead horses and military men scattered everywhere. Most had been scavenged and stripped of their supplies—boots and hats and guns and swords. All had been left to rot and stink under the hot southern sun. The field was plagued by an awful silence. It was as if the dead permitted no noise and the world around them complied with their demand.

The medic coughed and he spat.

The nun blessed herself and looked up toward the heavens.

"What won't men do?" the medic said.

"There ain't nothin men won't do," Maryellen said.

It happened like this. The small Tennessee town on the banks of the Mississippi had been subjected to a series of violent murders. Each day for a week a member of the local community was found scalped, tortured, propped up and displayed in a public place like some perverse statue or work of art. After the first two killings, rumors started to spread. Some said that a runaway slave had made his way back south in order to exact revenge on those who had kept him in chains. Some said that a small band of union soldiers were using guerrilla tactics to incite fear in the local community. Some said that the murders were ordered by Lincoln himself—that the man who had sacrificed his own son to demons in an effort to win the war was eager to sacrifice the sons of others. Some said that the killings would continue so long as the tyrant sat on his ivory thrown and demons were allowed to roam the earth with no masters and no restraints. Everyone knew about the bloodshed but no one knew what to believe. They were in a state of constant anxiety and their communal dread ate at them from daybreak to dark and deep into the night.

On Good Friday, a group of children found their school master nailed upside down to a yew tree near the old churchyard. The terrified townsfolk had had enough. They called on a regiment of confederate cavalrymen who made their camp a few miles up the road. The regiment was led by a Mississippi general of Scotch-Irish decent. He was a mean son of a bitch with thin red hair, a bushy red beard, and an inhuman appetite for violence. He rode into town on the back of a pale horse with a band of hellions close behind. He wore dated military regalia—relics of a forgotten time—and clenched the black end of a black cigar between his small, brown teeth.

"Well," he said. "You want my help—you do it my way."

The townspeople agreed.

That afternoon he rounded up every slave, servant, and invalid in the area and brought them to a nearby field. He even took the orphans and the town drunk. He marched them to the center of the field and questioned them one by one. When they did not answer or did not know how, he asked if they were aware that he had the power to set them free and the power to have them shot.

"Ya...ya...yer power's only the power a this world," one scared slave managed to stutter.

The general took his revolver from his belt and shot him clean through the head.

The slave's limp body buckled at the knees and it slumped forward and fell to the earth at his feet.

"Power a this world?" the general said. "What else is there?"

His men laughed and clapped and he proceeded to interview the next of his prisoners.

148

They spent the day doing this. Questioning the detainees and shooting them at will. They had taken a barrel of whiskey from one of the saloons in town and they drank and sang and slaughtered men like cattle. By nightfall they had few answers but they were having a good time for themselves so the festivities continued. Soon they made it into a kind of devilish game. They asked one young orphan if he loved them. He said, "Yes, I love you with my whole heart." They shot him through the chest for lying. They asked another orphan if he loved them. He said, "I ain't goin to lie. Truth is, I ain't love you a lick." They shot him through the chest for not loving them. One boy tried to run away. He sprinted off as fast he could. They sent their hound after him and watched as it closed in and tackled him screaming to grassy earth. They laughed as he kicked and flailed and screamed and screamed. He cried out for mercy and he cried out for god. But he received no answer.

It was those screams that garnered the attention of a union regiment stationed just up the road. They could hear the boy wailing in the dark and they sent their scouts to see what was the matter. When the scouts returned and told their general of the carnage, he ordered his troops to the ready.

"Savages," he said and he wiped his mouth. "Goddamned savages."

They set out under the moonlit sky with clubs and swords and bayonets fixed to their rifles. There would be war enough. Glory and battle and the taste of blood. But tonight had nothing to do with that. Tonight would be a butchering. A hot, brutal massacre. And there would be no reason in it at all. No reason but revenge. Revenge and meanness and a cold, bitter hate.

When the union soldiers came to the top of a small hill, they saw the field below lit up with firelight.

There were torches and bonfires and men drunk and singing. There were slaves in chains and young boys cowering in terror and bodies piled high, one atop the other. There was the smell of gunpowder and excrement in the air and there was a lone woman tied to a tree on the edge of the field. The confederates took turns beating her and abusing her and she had been so abused and torn up that she did not cry out but lay there motionless and defeated in the dark.

"Savages," the union general said. "Don't let one a them leave here alive. Not a single one."

The troops descended the hill in a furious charge but the confederates below were so drunk on whiskey and on the shedding of blood that they did not notice. They kept singing and clapping and when the union general rode through on horseback and began butchering them with his saber, they were stunned and almost thought him a part of their insane festival. His regiment followed close behind and the troops opened fire on the confederates and the dazed and blinking southerners were torn to pieces in the moonlight. There was blood and gunfire everywhere and in the chaos the confederate general pulled a knife from his boot and began stabbing soldiers at random — friends and enemies alike. He used his knife to pull the scalps off of the dead and he waved the scalps in the air and danced and sang and beat his chest.

The fighting continued to the morning and when it was finally over, the union soldiers had killed every confederate but one.

"This is their leader, sir," said a soldier to his general.

The man from Mississippi stood before him bruised and heaving with blood running down his face and patches pulled from his bushy red beard. He smiled an awful smile and his brown teeth were small and sharp like the teeth of an animal.

"What were my orders?" the union general said.

"Let no man leave here alive," the solider said.

"Strip him a that uniform," the general said. "He ain't fit to wear it. Tie him to a tree, fuck him til he can't stand, shoot him through the back, and leave him there to bleed out on the ground that he's stained with the blood a prisoners and children."

The soldier nodded and did as he was told and when he was done the regiment road off into the morning light.

❦

Maryellen found the pale and naked corpse of a man tied to a tree on the edge of the field. He had been shot clean through the back and had slumped down and bled out on the grassy earth. There were boot marks in the mud where his captor had stood behind him. His fingers were raw and bloody and there were chunks pulled out of the bark where he had scratched and clawed and pleaded for mercy. He had received none and it was clear to Maryellen that the bullet had not killed him instantly but that he had been alive for several hours bleeding and sniveling in the dirt. His jaw hung toothless and open and his rotten brown teeth were spread out on the damp sod. They had been pulled from his mouth one by one until his mouth was nothing more than a dark and gaping void in the center of his face. He was silent now but had spent the last hours of his life whimpering and moaning and praying for death. Death had come and there was mercy in that. Or if not mercy, finality. An end to the thing. A conclusion.

The simple desert nun, beautiful and modest, blessed herself and bent down next to the corpse. She wet her finger on her tongue and made the sign of the cross on the dead man's forehead. Then she placed her palm on his cold, lifeless face and closed her eyes. Tears ran down her cheeks and her hand began to shake. An expression of deep, sorrowful pain came over her and she looked like she might collapse. It was as if she had taken his suffering into herself and could feel the dark, wrenching loneliness of his death in her own body. She opened her eyes, fell to her knees, pressed her small, scarred hands into the dirt, and kissed the ground next to the dead man's feet. Then she untied his body, rolled it over stinking and decayed, and covered it with a simple, white cloth from a sack she had carried with her to the fields.

She stood, picked up her shovel, and began to dig.

❦

It was a dry morning in the summer of 1850 when Ignacio awoke in a Texas nunnery. His eyes shot open and he looked from side to side. He tried to sit himself up but could not move. His hands and feet were fastened to the bed, his body wrapped in bandages, his mouth dry and tasting of blood. He had sharp, shooting pains in his back and in his chest. His linens were damp, his body cold. There was sweat beading on his brow and a dull, aching pain in his jaw. He could not feel his fingers or toes and he had to look down at his body to make sure it was still there. He tugged at the restraints but could not break free. He blinked and looked around the room.

The sun broke in through windowless frames and there were icons and religious paintings on the walls. There was a picture of the madonna with child but the child was wounded and bleeding from his hands. There was an image of a saint on horseback carrying a flaming lance. He thrust it down through the face of an awful looking dragon and blood and fire poured from the dragon's mouth. There was a painting of a man with the body of a woman—breasts and hips and curves and all. He pulled open his chest in the middle and revealed a pierced and bleeding heart. There were candles and rose petals on a table in the corner, lilacs in a bowl by the door, and on the windowsill was a pot of fresh cut lilies as clean and as white as snow.

"Anticristo," muttered a haggard looking nun standing in the doorway.

Ignacio coughed and he tried to speak.

"Anticristo," she said and she spat on the floor.

"Water," he said. "Agua."

"Anticristo," she said and she crossed herself for protection.

"Out," said a second nun. "Vamonos."

She shooed the old woman away and entered the room herself. She was thin and beautiful with brown skin, black hair, and deep sorrowful eyes.

"Water," Ignacio said. "Water."

She fetched him a cup of water and he drank it down greedily.

"You've been unconscious for days," she said. "We weren't sure you'd ever wake up."

He coughed and tried to speak.

"Don't," she said. "Rest now. You'll need your strength to fight off infection. You were stabbed more than a dozen times. It's a miracle you're alive."

"How?" he said. "How did I get here?"

"Rest," she said. "There will be a time for questions. Your enemies are dead. You've destroyed them all. Rest now and when you awake the hour will come to seek forgiveness and to make amends."

He closed his eyes and offered himself over to a restless sleep.

She sat down next to him and read softly from the *Vita Christi*.

He shivered and his teeth chattered in his mouth.

She put down the book and stroked his hair.

He whimpered and she kissed him gently and he drifted off to sleep.

As he slept, Ignacio dreamt of the man from the painting, the man with the woman's body and full womanly breasts. He saw him from a distance with hair like lightning and clothing as white as snow. The man held a torch in one hand and a flaming sword in the other. And even though Ignacio feared him, still he felt that he had to approach. It was as if he had no say in the matter. As if the choice were not his. He was drawn to the man like a moth to the flame. But the nearer he drew, the more repulsion he felt. He was overwhelmed by an awful, wrenching dread. He covered his face with his hands and refused to look up. He tried to wake himself repeatedly but no matter what he did, he could not pull himself from the dream and a deep, piercing anxiety filled his heart. He fell to his knees before the man and began to weep uncontrollably. The man walked nearer still and Ignacio kissed the ground at his feet and hid his face in the dirt.

Then the man spoke. His voice was terrible and thundering like the voice of some brutal god. And though it was utterly alien and inhuman, still Ignacio recognized it. It was a voice as familiar as it was strange. A voice he had known from his youth. A voice like the voice of his mother. He had known it his whole life. And he would know until the day he died. And on the day he died, it would be the last voice echoing through him as he descended down into the dark.

"Arise," said the voice.

That was his only word.

※❀❀

It was early in the evening and Maryellen had been burying bodies all day. She and the medic had split up hours before and had taken different parts of the field. She liked to pray while she worked and if they had been near one another, he would have wanted to talk. He seemed to think he could scandalize her which was funny, she thought, considering the job at hand. He would talk about this patient or that and she found it odd that he seemed so struck by their weird and sinful behavior. It was as if he did not understand human beings at all. As if, for all his lessons in anatomy, he knew nothing of man's heart.

When Maryellen finished burying the naked and mutilated confederate corpse, she knelt down on the freshly turned earth and began to pray. Then she dug her fingers into the dirt and scooped out a small hollow with the cup of her hand. She poured some seeds into the hollow, spat on them, prayed, and covered them with the fertile soil. Someday, she thought, life will spring forth from this death. Birth from decay. Joy out of sorrow. Light breaking through the dark.

She rose to her feet, packed up her supplies, grabbed her shovel and her sack, and prepared to depart. Night had crept in without her noticing and it was dark and quiet. She heard crickets chirping in the wood and a lone owl called out from a nearby tree. She looked up at the sky, at the moon and the stars, and wondered what the future would bring. When she worked at ma'am's, she thought she would never escape. And when she lived with the desert nuns, she thought she would never recover. But here she was, a nun in her own right, and she had learned to trust that, as unpredictable as life could be, still it works toward some higher end. This life is not our own and we control nothing. In an odd way, the thought comforted her. She felt as if she could finally let herself go. As if she were in possession of some impossible good news that changed everything and made everything what it was. But more than that, she was filled with a strange, swooning sensation. A feeling of powerlessness. A feeling of loss. As if she were suspended out over a void and could be dropped at any moment. And she knew that the decision was not hers to make and that it had already been made.

She sighed and decided it was time to go. She was tired and sore, in need of a hot bath and a good meal. Her back ached and she had blisters on her hands and pruning on her feet. She scanned the field for her partner but could not see more than a few yards in front of her. The darkness was thick. It swallowed everything in sight. Suddenly, she heard a sound like music on the wind. It was someone playing a piano. But the noise did not come from the town or from the brothel down the road. Both were a ways off and the music was close. It came from the fields. As if it was just over the hillside. As if someone had rolled a piano out into the twilight and was playing there for the nameless corpses piled high and stinking under the moonlit sky.

She stood a while and listened in the dark. She wondered how it was possible. How had a piano ended up in the fields? Who had brought it there? Who was playing? And how did he know that song? Her song. The song she had learned as a child. She couldn't speak but broken Spanish, yet she knew every word.

She followed the noise into the darkness, forgetting about the medic and her plans to return to the town. She walked up the side of a small hill on the edge of the field and when she reached the top she saw a blazing fire and a man sitting on a stool playing the piano. There were wheel marks in the grass and dead bodies strewed across the damp sod. The man had wheeled the piano out at dusk and had built the fire to keep warm as he played. There was a nip in the air and he did not want to catch a chill.

Maryellen walked up behind the man and watched his fingers dance across the keys. He had black hair

and yellow eyes and his hands were stained red with
blood. As he played, she listened, fixed, trancelike. And
without knowing that she was doing it and without
knowing why, she sang along in a sad, hushed voice.

Qué linda manito que tengo yo,
Qué linda y blanquita que Dios me dio.
Qué lindos ojitos que tengo yo,
Qué lindos y negritos que Dios me dio.

The man's fingers leaped from one key to the
next—black to white and back again—and Maryellen was swept up in an ecstasy of sorrow and pain.

Qué linda boquita que tengo yo,
Qué linda y rojita que Dios me dio.
Qué lindas patitas que tengo yo,
Qué lindas y gorditas que Dios me dio.

The man sensed her presence and concluded his
song. Then he turned and looked at her with eyes
as black as marbles.

"Hello, mama," he said. "I've been lookin for you."

❧❧❧

She sat down next to the man and put her fingers
on the keys. It was clear she did not know how to
play so he put his hands on hers and guided them
to the right notes. There was water in her eyes and
teardrops rolled down her red, freckled cheeks. He
looked at her and grinned and he wiped the tears
from her eyes with his thumb. Then he removed the
black veil from her head and ran his fingers through
her hair. Her hair was reddish blonde and it was wavy.
It smelled like perfume powder and lavender and it
curled in the back. She was plain and beautiful with
freckles and ruddy cheeks. She wore a simple black
habit which covered her pale, white skin and she was
barefoot with little nub toes and white toenails. She
had deep, red scars on her wrists and on her feet and

157

she tried to hold back her tears but she could not and they fell from her eyes onto the wood of the piano.

"Don't be scared, mama," the man said.

"I'm not," she whispered.

"That's good," the man said. "Real good."

He moved her fingers up and down the keys and eventually her hands went numb and she could play no more so he lifted her hands off of the piano and placed them on her lap. Then he continued the song by himself, playing it masterfully. It was as beautiful as she had remembered and she closed her eyes and imagined the first time she had heard it. She was so little then. So unexpecting. And though at that point she had already lost much, still she had not understood what it meant to lose. And even today she was trying to understand.

When he was finished, he turned to her and said, "I was an orphan too."

She looked at him but could not find a hint of life behind his eyes, cold and black as they were.

"You don't remember me," he said. "The priest didn't either. But we all have that in common. You and me and the good Father Ignacio. All raised by them nuns. Him in Mexico. Us in Texas. We lost our parents to different demons—some less human than others. But we was all abandoned. All alone. And look where it got us. Look at how it all turned out. A priest. A nun. And the antichrist himself. Who would've ever guessed it?"

He paused as if thinking about that.

"You know," he said. "I ain't never told this to no one. But I trust you. After all, who can a man trust if not his mama?"

Her lip trembled.

"When I was a boy," he said. "Somethin happened. Somethin bad. Somethin I can't forgive."

She looked him deep in the eyes and he almost

looked like a boy now. Like he was trying to be a man but didn't know what that meant.

"When I was a boy—" he said.

Bang! Before he could finish a shot rang out. It tore through the back of the man's neck severing his head from his shoulders. Blood sprayed everywhere and his cold, lifeless body slumped forward onto the piano pressing down hard on the keys. A long, dead note continued to ring out and Maryellen screamed in terror. She turned and faced the gunman and saw the smoke still rising from the barrel of his Colt Model 1848 percussion revolver.

"You," she stammered. "I thought you was dead."

The altar boy looked at her over the barrel of his gun and he examined the dead man lying face down before him. He had been tracking this man for three years and had finally caught up with him. He kicked his body off of the piano and it fell to the ground with a thud.

"I swore you was," Maryellen said. "Figured he killed you and Father both."

"What're you doin here?" the boy said.

"I can't believe you're alive," Maryellen said. "Lord god, can't believe you're alive."

"What're you doin here?" the boy said. "What're you doin with him?"

"Why you lookin at me like that?" Maryellen said.

"You come here to forgive him?" the boy said.

"What's wrong with your eyes?" Maryellen said.

"You forgive that man?" the boy said. "After all he's done?"

"Somethin wrong with them eyes," Maryellen said. "Somethin ain't right about them eyes."

The boy was shaking. And though he had aged three years since she had last seen him, he was still a boy and his face was as pale as death.

Maryellen stood and reached out to touch him.

159

"Poor boy," she said. "Poor, poor boy."

He sprang back in revulsion and unloaded three slugs in her gut.

She fell forward and was dead before her body touched the ground.

"Forgiveness," the boy said, "is for god. The only thing a man can do is take his revenge."

THE END

EPILOGUE: EASTER MONDAY, 1917 ✺

It was on Good Friday 1917 that the United States House of Representatives joined the Senate in granting President Wilson his request for a Declaration of War. That weekend the young man spent time with his family. They talked about his course work and about the university baseball team and he went with them to church and ate a good Easter dinner which he followed with a slice of his mother's famous peach pie, a cup of black coffee, and a hand rolled cigarette for dessert. On Monday morning, his father dropped him at the train station and waited for him to buy his ticket before giving him a firm handshake and an extra 35 cents to buy a sandwich and a pack of smokes for the ride.

"Education," he said, "is your future. Don't you waste it."

"Yes, sir," the young man said and he watched his father leave.

Then he crumpled the ticket into a ball, threw it in a wastepaper basket, and left the station on foot. His grandfather lived nearby in a small house down a country road and he wanted to see him before going to the town hall to enlist.

When he got there, he knocked on the screen door but there was no answer. He stood on the porch next to his grandfather's old, wooden rocking chair and thought about what to do. Then he let himself in and walked down the long hallway which led to the bedroom.

"Pappy," he said. "You in there?"

There was no answer from within but he could hear the radio and thought that maybe his grandfather had fallen asleep.

He pushed open the door and entered.

"Pappy?" he said.

His grandfather was sitting on the edge of his bed listening to the day's news. They were reporting on the war effort and on the number of patriotic young Americans who were ready to enlist and even to die in order to preserve our freedom and the American way of life.

The young man looked at him intently.

"Pappy," he said. "What you doin in here?"

His grandfather turned and looked at him with pale, gray eyes.

"Pappy," he said. "What you doin with that gun?"

His hand was shaking. His brow was wet. He coughed and held out the gun and he looked at it as if surprised to see it in his hand.

"Pappy," his grandson said.

He had seen that gun before. Once, years ago, when he was a boy. His grandfather had left him in the house while doing work in the yard and he had taken the opportunity to go rummaging through his bedroom drawers. When his grandfather found out, he beat him with his belt. The beating was so severe that it left bruises for weeks and he never went rummaging again.

"Your pappy," his grandmother had said, "is a very particular kind of man. That gun is the one thing he kept from his time fightin to preserve this here union. He don't like to talk about the war or about what he had to do to keep this country whole and you best never ask."

The gun was a Colt Model 1848 percussion revolver. It had been fired before and god knows it would be fired again.

"The blood," his grandfather said, "ain't enough."

"Pappy," he said. "Why you lookin at me like that?"

"Thought it was," his grandfather said. "Thought

it might be. But it ain't. After all these years. It still ain't enough."

"Pappy," he said, "what's wrong with your eyes?"

"It's never enough," his grandfather said. "The blood ain't never enough."

"Pappy," the young man said, "there's somethin wrong with them eyes."

❧✿☙

In the cathedral downtown, a mass was being offered. It was Easter Monday and the priest was dressed in vestments white and gold. He performed the rituals in silence— blessing, consecrating, genuflecting, raising host and chalice high in the air, breaking the host into the chalice and preparing to consume. He chanted the "Agnus Dei" and as he did the laity rose from their pews and approached. They knelt at the stone altar rail and received the host on their tongues. And when the mass was over and the chanting was finished, they turned their backs on the altar and they walked out into the world.